Agatha and Frank

Road Trip Adventure

JOLYNN ROSE

Order this book online at www.trafford.com
or email orders@trafford.com

Most Trafford titles are also available at major online book retailers.

Print information available on the last page.

ISBN: 978-1-4907-6089-6 (sc)
ISBN: 978-1-4907-6090-2 (e)

Trafford rev. 06/03/2015

 www.trafford.com
North America & international
toll-free: 1 888 232 4444 (USA & Canada)
fax: 812 355 4082

Other books you may enjoy that have
been written by Jolynn Rose:

Roslander – The Island of the Merbeings

Roslanders – The Cities under the Sea

The Tales of the Merbeings Clans –

The Roslanders, Pagons and Imdom Clans

Agatha and Frank – Stranded on Rosland island

The Mystery of Dixie Mountain – by Lola Smith

DEDICATION

We want to dedicate this book to my sister and Mom's daughter Sharlene Smith-Pierce. She was a wonderful person and loved by all. Her passing was way too soon and she will be missed by all of us. I know she is up there with Dad and the rest of our family that has moved on.

Sharlene, Enjoy the other side!

PROLOGUE

After we spent five and half years stranded on Rosland Island, we were kind of rescued by the natives of Rosland, we called them the Roslanders. We had been living with the Roslanders, while we were on the island. The natives had found a boat that we used to leave the island, and helped us get to where other humans would find us. The time on the island was wonderful; the Roslanders took us into their clan, and taught us how to survive on the island. It was hard to leave the island, and the Roslanders. I think if it wasn't for our children and grandchildren we would of never came back.

I kept a journal of our time there, but it is time to make new memories with our family. I hope you enjoy our new adventures and maybe even learn a little history as we go along. Remember, I am a history teacher after all!

Aggie

CHAPTER 1

We have been back for five years and we have settled into the day to day life. We go out sailing as much as we can. Our kids join us on the boat whenever they can. They do have their own lives. We do enjoy it when we get the grandkids all to ourselves. With that said, we had all the six grandkids for a week on our boat. They were all wonderful and they enjoy listening to Grandpa and Grandma's Stories of our island adventures. Earlier, we were talking about going into the dream room on the island. How much we enjoyed going back to our family trips, when we were younger. The dream room is a place we found on Rosland Island. It was an ancient city, which had been covered up by the vegetation.

Anyway, this is when our oldest grandson Daniel asked, "Why don't Grandpa and you go visit those places for real? You promised each other you would!" Of course, Tina our oldest granddaughter had to join in and asked, "Why don't we all go?" The next thing we know all of the grandkids are cheering and agreeing with her. Grandpa wasn't any help, he agreed with them. Then Frank said "Let's make it a family trip, get a couple of RV's and see the site's of the United States. All the grandkids started cheering. I settled them all down and said we need to talk to your parents first. We don't know if they can take the time off. I thought to myself, there is no way I'm taking six kids across the country by myself.

For the rest of their visit, that is all the grandkids could talk about. Frank pulled out the maps we had of the United States, and was showing the kids, where we would be going. I just smiled and told him, you're going to have to talk to our kids. He smiled back and said, "How can they tell us no, we have been missing for five years. Funny, how Frank always uses that card, when he wants our kids to do something for us. I just smiled at him.

When we arrived back at the dock, our kids Frank Jr. (aka Frankie), Twila, and Maria, were waiting for us. Frank looked at me and said, "No time, like the present to talk to them." I had to agree; because I knew the grandkids wouldn't keep it a secret for long.

We asked our kids to come on board; we had something we wanted to talk to them about. First thing that came out of Twila mouth was "You're not taking off again, are you?" Well kind of, come on in and we'll tell you about our great idea.

CHAPTER 2

Our kids came into the cabin and I could tell by their looks, they were wondering what was on their crazy parents minds now? Frank Sr. started with "We have missed a lot of your lives, because we were stranded on Rosland for five and half years. It was hard on all of us, we missed so much!" Then Frankie spoke up, "Yea, we get it, so what is going on?" Frankie was a lot like his dad, he just wants to get to the point. I could see the grandkids, looking through the window, waiting to see what was going to happen. Then I took the lead, well we were telling the grandkids about the dream room. We told them how much we enjoyed going back to Utah and California and seeing where we used to go on vacation when we were young.

I could tell it was coming to them, what we were going to say. I passed it back to Frank Sr. Frank said, "The grandkids came up with a great idea." That's when all three turned around and saw all the kids looking through the window. They all waved and smiled; our kids turned around and waited for the bomb shell to drop. You have to remember Frank Sr. retired from the army, and the language has worn off on me and the kids. Maria finally asked, "What are you two up to?" Maria was like the both of us, hard but fair and enjoyed doing family things. I guess it was my turn again. We would like to go on a family vacation with the family on land! Normally, our vacations are on the water, we all have boats, and we would sail down to Florida or over to Mexico. We have never done a land vacation.

I wasn't surprised when Maria was the first to say "That is a great idea, I need to talk to James. I don't think it will be a problem, he hasn't had a vacation in years!" I gave her a big hug, and said that's my girl! Then Frank Sr. and I looked at the other two, waiting for them to say something. Frankie turned and looked at his boys, and they both were nodding their head yes. He turned back around and asked "How long? How are we traveling and what will be the cost?" Then Twila replied to Frankie "Good questions? I'll need the details so I can let Dennis know about our plans." Dennis was always up for adventure. He lived to make Twila happy and they both enjoy life, Dennis has been semi-retired for the last few years.

Frank Sr. told them "We would like to plan for a couple of weeks, maybe even a month. Our idea is to rent a Class a RV, from a friend of ours, and Maria and Twila already have trailers. We will use the RV as home base, and we can take turns driving the different vehicles. The good news is we'll pay for it all. We know you all can afford to pay your own way, just look at it this way; we are just spending your inheritance! I think that covers all of Frank Jr. questions! So what do you think?" Maria had one more question "When do you what to do this?" I replied, another good question, how about the middle of June? I have no clue why I picked June, but what the heck. It was mid May, so that will give us a month to get everything together.

It was the funniest thing; the kids looked at each other and then turned and looked at their kids. All of them were smiling and had their thumbs up and shaking their head yes! Our kids turned and Frankie spoke first, "I need to talk to Wanda, but I'm sure she will agree. She has been bugging me to take time off for awhile, we're in! It's been awhile since we have gone camping with the boys."

Then Maria said, "She needed to talk to James, but she was pretty sure he would be agreeable. James wanted to visit his family in Colorado anyway." Twila ended the agreement with "What the heck, if Dennis is ok with it, were in too! All the grandkids started cheering and jumping up and down. We couldn't help but laugh and started cheering to. We all went out to the deck and hugs all around. Now the hard part getting everything ready, good news is this is what Frank loves to do. By the time he's done, he'll have every minute accounted for! Here we go on a new and hopefully wonderful adventure.

CHAPTER 3

The first thing Frank did is go to a gas station and get all maps of the states we were planning on going through, he also pick up a United States map. I called AAA and asked for information on the areas we were going to travel. The new freeway they put in will make it a lot nicer to travel on.

I know one of the things we want to see is the cavern they have opened up to the public a couple of years ago. The first one isn't too far from here, it's called Inner Space Cavern; it's about a two and half hour drive. It was found by accident while they were putting in the new freeway. According to the newspapers "The highway department was doing test core drillings in 1963. They did the test sample to ensure the ground would be stable enough to support the new highway. As they were drilling one of the test holes, the drill bit suddenly dropped 26ft. and the highway crew knew there was something besides rocks.

They first opened it up to spelunkers in November 1963; they investigated the cavern even more. Then in the summer of 1966 they opened it up to the rest of the public." Being a retired history teacher, I love all the little detail. On Rosland Island, there was so much history. I had no clue where everything came from, because we were so isolated there. That is one of the reasons why we were so anxious to explore the island.

We don't know how much the kids will like going to the cavern, but with all the things the Roslanders told us about the different minerals; that they have discovered in the cavern around the islands. We wanted to see them first hand. Who knows maybe we'll take a trip up to Inner Space Cavern, before we go on vacation with the kids, to make sure it is interesting.

Frank and I talked about it, and decide we didn't have anything else to do, so we told the kids that we were going to head up to the Cavern to check it out. We were just going to make a day of it. The next thing we knew everyone was going and we were going to spend the weekend up there. Maria said, "Nothing like a test run, if we can't make it for two days, how are we going to make it for a month!" Now everyone is going, so I asked our friend Linda if we could use the RV for the weekend. She said, "Sure, it's a good idea to try it out before you head out on your journey.

I was standing in the RV looking around. I was thinking everything you need in a home away from home. As I was getting instruction from Linda, I thought one thing is missing. I asked Linda what was the RVs name. She said it doesn't have a name. She told me I could name it, if I wanted too.

Well I sure did, it was my thing. I would need a little help. I'll get the grandkids to help. I got them all together and told them what we were going to do; we are going to name the RV. Each one of them was to write a name down on a piece of paper and put it in grandpa's old cap.

They thought it was great fun, until they tried to come up with a good name. Finally we all came up with names. They were Annabelle, Tweedy, Toad, Seamore, and Tofoo.

I was thinking maybe this wasn't such a good idea. Too late they had them all in the cap and were ready to draw. Of course, grandma got to draw. As luck would have it I drew my own donation which was Seamore. To my surprise they all liked it. Maybe they just wanted to get back to their own business. Great then, Seamore it is!

Everything was set, Saturday morning we all loaded up and headed on our trip. We had purchased hand radios for each of the vehicle, which of course we had to test a few times. All of the grand kids wanted to ride in the RV, of course! The two and half hours went by pretty fast for me and the grandkids. We played games and had a coloring contest, and had some snacks. This is the only way to travel with kids. We got loud a few times and Grandpa in his military voice would call back "Settle down back there." Then told me if I couldn't behave I would have to come up front and sit down. All of the grandkids thought that was so funny.

We finally arrived at our camp site, it was just a small camp ground, but it was clean and had a play ground and a pool. We all unload and the kids ran over to the play ground and started to play, it was noon, while the men set up camp, us ladies made lunch. We only had to call the kids once, to come and eat. I think they were a little hungry. After we cleaned up and put everything away, we headed over to Inner Space Cavern.

This will be the first time any of us have been inside a cavern. We just took the two cars, to the Cavern. I'm sure it looked funny, all of us piling out of the cars. The building to the cavern wasn't very big, I guess it just needed to cover the entry way. When we purchased the tickets they told us we should wear our jackets, it can get cold in the cavern. Lucky we had ours in the car; for once it wasn't too warm out.

The way you had to get down into the cavern, was interesting. The seats looked a lot like rollercoaster seats, but bigger, it went down on rails until it came to a stop. It took us down to the bottom of the hole very slowly into the cavern, which only took three minutes. Then we all unloaded and waited for the next load of people.

The tour guides waited for everyone to settle down and told us to gather around, so we could get our flashlights and instruction on what we can and cannot do in the cavern. The little ones started getting a little scared and they grabbed their parent's hand.

The guide started leading the way and we all got in a line and followed him. As we went down the path, there were lights showing us the way. In the beginning there wasn't much to see, but as we moved farther into the cave, it opened up into a large room. It was all lit up and you could see huge stalactites and stalagmites, it was awesome. When we first went into the cavern, we saw soda straws hanging from the top of it. Of course, they weren't really soda straws, but they sure looked like them, it is what they called them. I guess you could call them baby stalactites'.

As we walked deeper into the cavern, you could see what looked like mudslides, but they called them flow stones. We even were allowed to touch one of them, but were told to not touch any others. The flowstones were hard but slippery, it was hard to tell the color, but it looked kind of light orange. The guide told us, that the oil from our skin can kill the growth of the stone. Then the guide pointed out the area where people have been touching the stone, in the past. It was black, and felt like a normal rock.

The grandkids were ohhhing and ahhing, and wanted to go touch them. We noticed that little Treva had gone under the rope and was heading towards the stones. James ran after her and pulled her back on to the path. Treva started crying and yelling she wanted to touch the pretty rocks. Maria explained, "That if she touched the rocks, she could make the stones sick." Treva said, "Oh, I don't want to hurt them, and she stopped crying.

The guide told everyone, please hold on to your child, we would hate to see them get hurt! As we went along we saw pools of clear water, and you could see your reflection in it. Twila said "I can even see the zit on my face, from the reflection in the water!" The cavern went on for miles, but wasn't open yet to the public, we saw the first mile. The guide told us that they had discovered a lake five miles inside the cavern. How cool would that be to see!

The guild told everyone to gather around in this one large room. Then he told us "I'm going to turn off the lights, please don't turn on your flashlights. When you close your eyes its dark, but you don't know what is dark until we turn off the light. It will only be a few seconds, and I will turn the lights right back on. He turned to James and said, "Everyone please hold on to your children." James smiled, and grabbed Treva's hand and

Maria grabbed Enola. I grabbed Franks hand; I wasn't going to take any chances.

He turned off the lights, and it was quite an experience to have your eyes open, and see total darkness. I was thinking to myself, it got black on the island at night sometimes, but nothing like this. He turned the lights back on and the first thing everyone did, is turn to see if Treva was there. Good news, everyone was there, Enola looked like she didn't understand what happened, because everyone was amazed at how dark it could get.

At that point the guide turned us around and headed us back up to planet earth. The roller coaster seats weren't as fast going up as it was coming down. So far so good, well we didn't lose anyone, and it sounded like everyone had a great time.

After we returned to camp, the guys started a campfire, and the kids helped move the picnic table's around the fire. Once the fire was going, we threw some steaks and hot dogs on the grill, for dinner. Frank and I can never get enough steak! I had made my potatoes salad the night before; all we had to do is make the green salad. We stood around talking about the cavern, everyone enjoyed it. We agreed that we would plan on seeing a couple more on our trip. We got out the cards and each table played different games. It had been a long day so everyone turned in pretty early. Tomorrow we will be heading back home to Houston.

Well the plan was to head back home in the morning, but things changed. Frank Sr. (aka Grandpa) wanted to go to Ft. Hood, we were stationed there and he wanted the grandkids to see where we used to live. All he had to say there are tanks and big truck's you can climb on. Grandpa knew how to get the grandkids on his side. It was only 50 miles from where we were. We left the RV's at the campground and we will pick them up on the way back. We packed a lunch, and loaded up the two cars. Again I felt like we were doing a clown act. If you don't know it can get pretty hot in Texas, so you travel in the morning and hopefully get to where you want to go by noon. One nice thing about being the Grandma, I get to ride in the front seat. I don't even have to call "Shot gun!"

After stopping for a bathroom break, we arrived at Ft. Hood; it had grown a little from the last time we were there. It started out as Camp Hood in 1942, and continues to grow with each war. Fort Hood is where Frank and I first met. We were both in the same division, but I met him at a friend's party. So we have a lot of history here. We took the kids to the museum first, we figured they could run around, climb on the different vehicles. The museum wasn't very big, but there were lots of tanks and trucks to climb on.

After a little bit, we went to the park area and had lunch. After lunch we rode around and showed the kids where our barracks were and the motor pool where we worked. After the grand tour we headed back to the camp ground. It didn't take long to get back to camp. Once we got back to camp; the kids went off to play.

Daniel asked us, "Why we had joined the Army." I told him, I think it because both our fathers had been in the Army, they had been in WWII. Dad "Lazelle" didn't say much in the beginning about what happen to him in Germany, (European theater). But after I went into the Army and married Frank who was also in the Army, he started to open up to us.

I guess he felt he could talk to us about what he saw. He saw a lot of horrible things while he was there. He was in five major campaigns (battles) in Germany. If it wasn't for a spike in the road he might have been killed.

His company was one of them that were getting ready to go into Berlin, when they were told to stop. They were told to let the Russians take Berlin first. Like most American soldier back then they lived thought the hell, and were expected to go back to a normal life. As we grew up he had his bad days and good days. But I think it was his music that kept him going. He loves to play his banjo and fiddle with his friends. Well that and the love of a great women, my Mom. She married Dad at 15, and never looked back.

Grandpa Frank's Dad (Dennis) was younger but he went to Japan. He would say "To kick some ass!" He had to take a ship over to Japan, so it took a little while to get there. On the way over to Japan the war ended. He always said, "They gave up because they knew he was coming." He also told us it wasn't a pretty site as they went into the Tokyo bay. It was thick with overturned ships and the fuel oil stood a foot deep on top of the water. As they got closer to land the water was red with blood, bodies everywhere.

They had to secure and clean up an area, so they could set up a command post for the America officers. The Japanese soldiers that were capture were put to work building things. He had a Japanese crew assigned to him, as a work crew. Most of the America soldiers treated them ok, but there was one First Sergeant that would beat on them and push them around. Dennis didn't like the way he was treating them. He asked him not to do it, and one thing led to another and Dennis knocked the Sergeant on his ass, and Dennis was busted down to private again.

Grandpa Lazelle got out when his time was up, but Dennis made a career out of the Army. I guess that why Grandpa Frank and I went into the Army. We wanted to serve our country too! One thing our Dad's agreed on is it was an Honor to Serve! We feel the same way, I served six years in the Army, but supporting my husband was a lot harder than being in the services sometimes.

Wanda and Twila are ready to head out. I smiled at Daniel and said any other questions? He said, "Yes, but I think I'll ask Great Grandpa Lazelle and Dennis about it."

As I was telling Daniel about his grandfather, he and Tina helped us to get the RV ready to go. We had to put things away inside and out. This was our first time breaking down camp, so we wanted to make sure nothing was left out. Linda (the owner) made us a check list, which was a big help. As Tina and I was putting everything up inside, I could hear the kids playing war in the play ground. I'll never get tired of hearing the kids laugh while playing.

Frank Sr. and I used to go to this steak house call Shirley Steak House. It was wonderful, it was a flour mill at one time, and they remodel it into a restaurant. Talk about country, when you go in you feel like you're in the 1940's, all kinds of things on the wall and the salad bar was in a bath tub, and the drinking glasses were mason jars. The steaks were huge and cooked on a Bar BQ out back. We wanted to take the kids there! Which we did, the grandkids didn't understand why we were drinking out of canning jars, and why there was a bathtub in the middle of the restaurant. But they did like all the cool things on the wall, they kept asking what was that used for, or can I touch this. Having six kids in a restaurant may not have been our best idea, but we had a great time with them. The owner even came to our table and told them a story about how the mill was an important part of their town. Of course, Sharlene asked him, "Did you work there?" He smiled and said, "No it was a little before my time, but my Grandpa and Dad did. She smiled and just said "Oh!" After dinner we loaded back up, this time the kids rode in the RV, so they could sleep on the way home. It didn't take them very long to fall asleep; all of them were out within 15 minutes.

We arrived back home and decide to let all the kids sleep, we woke up Daniel and Tina. We told them we were home, and to keep an ear out for the kids. All we got out of them was "Sure!" We were parked at Frank Jr. house, so they were pretty safe anyway. We all went into Frank Jr. and Wanda's house and had a cup of coffee and talked about our next adventure. Frank Sr. began, "I have all the maps and I have circled areas where there is camp grounds and places to stop and check out. What I need from you is to check and see if there is anywhere you want to stop. Your mom has gotten all of these flyers from AAA, if you want I'll go get them from the house." The kids agreed, but Maria said, she would go get them, just tell her where they are, Frank did and off she went.

Maria returned with the box of information, and our kids started looking at them. The more they looked the more they were getting excited. We talked about the different places and made plans. A one way trip to the Redwood National Forest in California was 2605 miles; we agreed we would go up through Davis, OK and then head to Colorado, Utah, and Nevada and then last stop the Redwood forest in CA.

On the way back we'll go down through Nevada, Arizona, New Mexico and then across Texas. There is so much to see and do in this wonderful country of ours.

It was pretty late before we headed to bed. Twila went out and checked on the kids, everyone was sound asleep before too long. I'm pretty sure it won't take me long to fall asleep. Frank is already sleeping. But I wanted to write in my journal before I forget anything.

Our first leg of our adventure,
Houston, TX to the Redwood Forest National Park in CA.
Come join us on our travels across the USA!

CHAPTER 4

Day 1
Davis, OK

I haven't been writing in my journal too much, we have been getting ready for our trip. All of our kids are taking off a month from work. We have drawn out our trip on the map and have all the supplies loaded. Each of our kid's family had picked out a place they would like to stop on the way. All the grandkids can talk about is the trip. We will be traveling with the RV, two trailers, and they are bringing two tents. We will be buying food as we go, it doesn't make sense to carry any more than we need to. Of course, we filled all of the water tanks, and propane tanks.

Only seven more days and we'll be off, I'm looking forward to seeing my home state of Utah again. Frank has been talking a lot more about the things his family used to do. His Dad was also a military man and they did a lot of traveling while he was in the Army.

Well today is the big day, the whole week has been checking and double checking. Looking at maps, and brochure of all the places we are going to stop. It's going to take longer than a month; we'll just have to go with the flow! We all agreed to meet at the rest area outside of town on Woodall Rodgers Freeway.

Everyone was waiting on us at the rest area, all the grandkids wanted to ride in the RV with us. How could we say no? I don't think their parents were to upset about it either, they all had big smile on their faces, and gave us a thumps up. I'm beginning to hate that sign. Everyone loaded up and we headed out on our new adventure. Time went by pretty fast; I sat up front with Frank and watched the landscape go by.

When we arrived at Davis, OK! It looks like a great place to visit, as usual I love noting the history about each place we stop. According to the visitor's center, Davis is just one town in Oklahoma who "owes its existence to the Santa Fe Railway. There are trains that still use the railway that runs through the middle of Davis. Davis is named after Samuel H. Davis who moved to Washita in 1887, he married a Chickasaw woman." We stopped and visited the Turner Falls Park, it was beautiful, and "it is the oldest park in Oklahoma, according to the sign." There is so much to do, they even have a castle, but we are only here for the day, and we all agreed to go to the Pow Wow.

Correction on the bathroom remark earlier! When I went to get lunch ready, I found an inch of water on the floor. I went to the bathroom and water was coming out of the top the toilet. I kicked the foot pedal and it stopped. One of the kids had used the toilet and the pedal had gotten stuck, and let the water run, so not only did we have 20 gals of water on the floor, we don't have any fresh water now. Of course, everyone had to come in and see what had happened. I told everyone lets have lunch and then I will clean it up. I suggested that everyone to go to the Pow Wow and I would join them as soon as I got everything cleaned up. Enola and Treva wanted to help, so I said it was ok. They did a great job, I put a rag down and they pushed the water down the steps. I mopped and we all sang to the radio, then we joined everyone at the Pow wow.

The little ones wanted to know what a Pow Wow was. I explained to them, "Pow Wows are the Native American people's way of meeting together, to join in dancing, singing, visiting, renewing old friendships, and making new ones. This is a type of method to renew Native American culture and preserve the rich heritage of American Indians." I read this off a flyer earlier today. One of the ladies at the visitor center told us, "There are several different stories of how the powwow was started. Some believe that the War dance Societies of the Ponca and other Southern Plains Tribes were the origin of the powwow. Another belief is that when the Native American tribes were forced onto reservations. The government also forced them to have dances for the public to come and see." I love history!

We joined everyone at the Pow Wow, this is our first Pow Wow; it was wonderful to see all the different tribes in their native clothing. I missed the beginning but I asked one of the ladies that were standing next to me, what was going on, she said, "There are several tribes gathered here, they each share their songs, dances and stories. Only the tribe member can join in and must be in their native clothing. But there are dances that everyone can join in."

I was watching the younger kids, dancing to the music and trying to dance like the tribe members were doing. After a little while all of us joined in. The kids were great; they acted like they knew what they were doing. Frank and I ended up stopping and watching them. It was a lot of fun for us to watch. Twila and Dennis were really getting into it. After the dance we walked around the market area.

We walked around and there was table after table of items the natives had made. The four youngest all wanted a head dress, Daniel and Douglas wanted an ax, and Tina wanted a head band. We ladies all purchased necklaces and bracelets. The guys got man bracelets; it was a leather band with markings on them.

This was only our first day; we need to slow down on our souvenir collecting. I think everyone had a good time, until we got out into the parking lot. We heard this man yelling at this woman in a car. She was trying to back up into a space between two cars. He kept telling her, "It is ok come on back." Both of them had been drinking too much, by the sound of it. Anyway, she started backing up and she hit the car on the right side, then she turned the car too much and hit the car on the left. She continues to back up, and hit the cars a couple of more times. Well she did get the car in to the space! When she tried to get out of the car; she had to climb out the window. Then they walked off laughing and went over to the Pow Wow. We all just looked at each other in shock.

After watching the show in the parking lot, we headed back to the camp ground. We did stop and tell the parking attendant about what happened; he thanked us for letting him know. We had been told earlier by the camp host, that there will be a bonfire later that night, at the back part of the park. We had a couple of hours to kill, so we had dinner and then the guys decide to go down to the bar down the street and have a couple of beers and play some pool. The older grandkids, wanted to go swimming and the little ones wanted to play at the park, which was right across from our campsite. Us ladies sat outside and had some wine and watched the kids play. Then of course we had to get out the cards and play a couple hands. While we gals were playing cards, we had time to just talk. The guys were off doing whatever guys do at a bar. It was Maria's turn to scuffle. Twila piped up and asked me if I would mind if she asked me a personal question. I replied, no go ahead. With a shy look on her face she said, "I was wondering what you did about your period while you were on the island?" I told her, it wasn't really a problem at all, since I started my menopause in my late forties. Twila said "Oh, you don't look that old mom, I should have known that." We all laughed. I thanked her and we got on with the game. It set me to wondering, did the mermaids have periods. We had never disgusted that. I would assume they did, all other life does or do they?

Just like clockwork, at 8:30 everyone started coming back to the camp site. We had agreed earlier that we would all meet here and go over to the bonfire together. We all headed over to the bonfire, what a group. I think the guys had a really good time at the bar. I guess Dennis won money and drinks playing pool. When we arrived at the bonfire it looked like everyone from the campground was there.

In the beginning it was great, they had a band playing country music and they had a dance area. Everyone was out dancing; even the little ones were joining in. Then they lit the bonfire, it was huge. From what I was told they have one every month here, during the summer. Everyone in the surrounding area is welcome to bring their wood debris. It was the first one of the summer. I guess there was a lot of debris to bring in.

As the night went on, the drunks took over the party so it was time for the grandkids to go to bed, besides we had to get up early. We could see the bonfire from the RV; it looked like it was getting a little crazy over there. The fire was getting smaller and the music had changed from the native songs they were playing when we left to a variety of music. Some of it, I couldn't recognize!

Our first day down and only 29 days to go! The guys slept in the tents. Frank and I slept in the RV. The gals and the little ones, all slept in their trailers. I guess we'll see how everyone's slept in the morning.

CHAPTER 5

Day 2
Santa Rosa, NM

Our second day on the road, after getting everyone fed, it took a little while to break down everything. James had stated earlier, it was hard for them to sleep in the tent because of all the noise coming from the bonfire. Around 11 o'clock, he heard the host settled everyone down and then they got some sleep.

As we were pulling out of the campsite, Dennis called on the walkie-talkies. He told Frank Sr. that we had forgotten to put the TV antenna and the air vents down. I got up and lowered everything, as we were heading down the road. That is one nice thing about having a rig where you can get up and go into the back area! I also added them to our checklist; the list is getting really long!

23

Our next stop is Santa Rosa, New Mexico, it's about 502 miles, and it's mostly prairie, so there is miles and miles of nothing to see. Santa Rosa is a nice little town; we have stopped there a couple times when we would go see my parent's in Utah. One of the cool things with Santa Rosa it has many natural lakes, which is unusual for a dry desert climate that surrounds it. They were sinkholes that were formed in the limestone bedrock at one time and filled up with water. We are going to stop at the campsite by the Blue hole, and maybe do a little bit of diving; it is over 81 feet deep.

Here's a little bit of history from the brochure we picked up from the visitor center. "The first European settlement in the area in 1865, was Aqua Negra Chiquita, in Spanish it means "Little Black Water. They changed the name to Santa Rosa in 1890 (Spanish for "Holy Rose") referring to a chapel that Don Celso Baca (the founder of the city) built and named after both his mother Rosa and Saint Rose of Lima. The "Rosa" may also refer to the roses in the story of Our Lady of Guadalupe and is indicative of the Catholicism of the Spanish colonizers who settled in the area." There is so much history in this area, I'm sure there have been many books written about the area. But we love stopping here, because of how friendly the people are here.

We have been on the road for about three hours and everyone is getting a little restless. We saw a sign saying "Café one mile." I pointed to the sign and told Frank, I think everyone must be getting hungry by now. How about stopping for lunch Frank? Frank said, "Ok, give the kids a call on the radio and let them know we are stopping for lunch." I called the kids on the walkie talkie and asked them if they wanted to stop and eat. They replied "Yes, please!"

As we pulled in, it looked like there were not very many customers. Thank goodness, we had quite a crowd; there were fourteen of us, all together. I noticed the owners were quite pleased to see us. They even put some tables together to accommodate us.

As we were setting down, Grandpa Frank took off for the rest room. The waitress came over to take our orders, so I ordered for Frank too. He always orders the same thing anyway, cheese hamburger with lots of mustard and onions, of course a side of fries.

Frank seems to be taking awhile, when Wanda turned to me and asked, "Who is that man dad is talking too? I replied, who knows, he's always talking to strangers. He gets some interesting information that why.

Finally when he got back to the table, we were all waiting to hear what he had found out. He sat down and looked at all of us and asked "What?" Then he smiled and told us that the guy has lived in this area his whole life. He was telling me there is a ghost town not far from here, which we might like to check out. The people in town don't tell everyone about it because they think it is haunted. The guy that owns it doesn't want people messing around out there. The people, who own it, don't want a lot of people going up there and destroying the town. James asked, "Frank how come he told you?" Frank replied, "I told him we would only stop for a short time, and about our family trip. I guess he liked my looks!"

"Anyway, we go eight miles on this old dirt road and there it is. It wouldn't take long for us to just to check it out. The old guy said, we could leave our RV and trailers around back and come back and pick them up after." Frank explained. Of course, the grandkids were listening to every word, and they all started cheering and saying can we, can we! Grandpa did his look and everyone got quite. I guess we're going to a ghost town.

It was a warm summer day, perfect for an adventure. It didn't take long to find the ghost town. It was surrounded by nothing but high desert. There were tumble weeds on the semi road going through the ghost town. We pulled into what would be called the center of town.

When we all got out of the cars, Frank said, "We should all stay together. No telling what we will run into!" We all gathered together, the little ones grabbed their parents hands, the older grandkids hung out with Frank and me.

The wind started blowing the tumble weeds around, they acted like they didn't want us there, and we had to get out of the way of a few of them. It felt like they were attacking us.

We went into the hotel first; the porch was rotten in places. The lobby was dusty and smelled musty. Although it was sunny outside, it was dark inside; there were dirty rotten drapes on the windows. There was a register desk at the back side of the lobby, with shelves behind it. There was also some broken furnisher and a door leading into a lounge.

The younger grandkids wanted to go upstairs, but the steps were all rotten. They lost interest and wanted to see the saloon next door. Maria leaned toward me and whispered "Don't you think this was the whore house?" It might have been, I replied. Frank said, "Come on gang to the saloon. Frankie smiled and said "Now you're talking!"

The wind was getting stronger now, and was kicking the dust up on the road as we walked out of the hotel. It was starting to feel like a ghost town. We had to be very careful now, the steps and porch of the saloon was disintegrating! As we entered the saloon, all I could think of was the western towns on television. Inside it was dark and dirty, but it had an eerie feeling. The bar was along one end of the room. There were a few tables and chairs, which were in need of repair. One table was larger than the rest; it looked like the poker tables we use to see in the movies.

Behind the bar there were some shelves and there was a space where there was once a mirror. You could still see a piece still in it place on the wall. The other pieces of the mirror were all around on the floor. As we stood there all grouped together there was a cold draft. I didn't understand it, because it was warm when we first enter the saloon and it was getting hot outside. None of us felt very comfortable in the saloon.

Even the younger kids were all still, which was a wonder in itself! It was like we were waiting for something to happen. There was a back room and the door was partly open. Frankie wanted to take a look in the room, he took his boys with him, and they weren't gone too long. When he came back he said, "Not much back there, just a broken down cot with a rotten mattress. There were a couple empty whiskey boxes, a demolished desk and an old empty safe. It must have been the owner's office and storage room."

As they joined the rest of us, we decided maybe we should get back on the road. As we started to leave, I glanced up at the broken mirror behind the bar. I let out a scream; there in the mirror was an image of someone who looked like an old cowboy. The others turned when I screamed, but he already started to fade away, and then he was gone. I pointed at the mirror and asked did you see him. Twila said, "Mom, see who? There is no one there!"

All I knew was I had to get out of there. As we were standing out in the road, I told them I saw a ghost. No one knew what to say, and just padded me on my back, telling me it is ok. Then we heard this moaning, it first sounded like the wind, but then it sounded like someone in pain. Frank told us to stay put, and Frank and Frankie would go check it out. James and Dennis stayed with us, just in case something weird is going on. I told Frank to take a walkie talkie, and keep us updated. Frankie grabbed the radio, and they headed toward the noise. As they were walking away, I did a radio check. Frankie turned around and said "Yes, Mother we can hear you!" I replied, Roger that, and we all waved at them.

All we could do is wait now. After about five minutes, Frank came over the radio. Aggies are you there? I replied back, yes what did you find? He replied back, "We found an injured man, bring the first aid kit, we're behind the stable." I replied back, on our way! Maria had already ran to the car and got the kit. Everyone had to go and see the injured man. I told the grandkids to stay behind their parents, just in case. I didn't have to tell them twice, they moved behind their parents. As we rounded the corner there stood the guys, there was a man on the ground. It looked like he had a head injury, I handed Frank the first aid kit. He helped the man sit up and had him drink some water. According to his story, his name was Jake, and he and his friends had robbed a bank, and we're hiding out in the stable until they stopped looking for them. The next thing he knew he was laying there bleeding from his head. Frankie helped him up and said we would take him to the café down the road. He agreed he wanted to turn himself in and turn the dirty rats in, that were part of the robbery. They had left him there to die!

We agreed that the women and kids would all ride in the van, and the guys would ride back in the other car with Jake. We didn't need the kids being around him. He looked familiar, as we were loading in the van it hit me; it's the cowboy ghost I saw earlier. I didn't tell anyone, I wasn't sure how they would take it. Maria was driving, as I rode shot gun as usual! As we started down the road, we went past the city limit sign, then all of a sudden the guy's slowed their car down, and they started honking. I could hear James voice over the radio, telling us to stop. Maria stops the van, and I jumped out of the van to see what had happened.

The guys were out of the car and were looking underneath and around it. I asked them, what are you doing? Dennis said, "Jake is gone, he disappeared! He started looking bad, and then he just faded." Frank didn't see anything; all he heard was Dennis saying "What the hell, where did he go!" Frank turned to ask him who, and he saw Jake was gone. It was crazy for a few minutes while we all tried to understand what had happen. Then I saw the city limit sign, and I suggested maybe Jake couldn't leave town. He was the cowboy I saw in the mirror in the saloon. Frank asked, "Why didn't you tell us? I just said, "Guess!"

Twila piped up and said let's go back to the café and talk to that old guy, Dad was talking to earlier. We all agreed and loaded up and headed back to the café. Twila and Maria said, "They would go get the trailer hooked up while we went and talked to the old man." Good idea, the grandkids were already asking about Jake, and where did he go.

Frank and I went into the café, but the old guy wasn't there. The waitress came up to us, and said "Welcome back, where is the rest of the family?" Frank told her they were hooking up the trailer in the back. Then Frank said, "I was talking to an old guy when we were here before. Is he around?" She said. "You must be talking about old Chris. He was here a little while ago. He must have went around back, she pointed to the back door. "You can go that way." We thanked her and headed out the back door.

When we went out back, old Chris was talking to our kids. Frankie waved at us, as we were walking towards them; Chris turned and had a big smile on his face. Then he turned to Frank and said "I told you it was a ghost town!" We weren't sure if we should be upset or not. Then Frankie spoke up "That is true, Dad!" We couldn't help but laugh. Frank agreed with them. I had to ask, so what is the story about Jake, and what happened to him? Why can't he leave the town?

Old Chris said "Well, the story goes back to 1896 Jake and his two buddies robbed the town bank. As they tried to leave the town, the town folks caught them by the stables. Jake was running when someone hit him from behind and killed him. His two friends were hung up on the limb of the old tree outside of town. I guess they assumed that Jake was dead, so they just left him there to rot. Then he was buried with the other two robbers behind the stable.

This is the story that has been passed down. Every time someone spends time in the ghost town, Old Jake tries to escape to the town. He always tells the same story to the people that find him. But this is the first time he ever got into a car with anyone. Frankie smiled and said "I guess we were just lucky!"

Frank and I have no problem believing pretty much everything these days. All the things we found and seen on Rosland, anything is a possible. We thanked Old Chris for the interesting time, but we needed to get back on the road. The grandkids are ready to start the next adventure; they were all sitting in the car waiting for us.

The grandkids have been doing pretty good considering what had happened earlier, but this is Route 66 and there are many ghost stories on this road.

Twila and Dennis took the lead this time. We have another couple of hours before we reach Santa Rosa, we are only going to spend the night there and then head back out on the road. We hope to get some swimming in this evening at the camp grounds, but you never know. We are water people; we all enjoy a good swim in the evening.

It took us three hours to get to Santa Rosa. Maria and James trailer got a flat tire. Of course, there was nowhere to pull off the road, to change the tire. They had to stay on the road, which was only a two lane road. We parked the RV behind them and Twila and Dennis stopped at the first pull off. Frankie and Wanda had stopped in front of James and Maria. We had called them on the walkie-talkies and told them what had happened. Maria and the grandkids went out into the desert and looked for rocks while James and Frankie worked on getting the tired changed. The nuts on the wheel were really tight.

We watched James stand on the lug wrench and jumped up and down, trying to loosen the nuts. Wanda came back to see if there was anything they could do. James said "No." Wand said, "She had talked to Twila on the walkie talkie and they had found a pull off about a half a mile away. Wanda offered to take the kids with them; she was going to pull the van up to the pull off too. Maria said, "That would be great!" The girls were complaining there wasn't anything to do. They had a handful of rocks; but they weren't allowed to go into the trailer with them.

As James was jumping up and down on the lug wrench, he said "Yeah that would be great, agreeing with Maria!" Wanda and Maria grabbed the girl's and headed to the car. Every time, James got one lug nut loose, he called out "Another one down, only two to go, and so on."

Every time a big truck went by the trailer, the trailer would go back and forth. I held my breath, it looked like the trailer was going to fall off and go down the hill. The Franks put their hands on it, as if they were trying to stop it from rolling over. I would warm them, every time a big truck would be coming down the road. After 45 minutes the tire was changed, and we could join the other kids. The rest of the trip to Santa Rosa was uneventful. Thank goodness!

We pulled into the campground and set up our campsites and decided to have pizza for dinner that night. We ended the day with a swim in the pool and it was game night at the rec. center. We ordered the pizza and played games until nine. We all were pretty tired tonight, it was quite the day.

Next stop is Cortez, Colorado; we are planning on spending a couple of days in southern Colorado, before we head up to see my family. It's been a while since I've seen my family; they all came down to Houston, when we returned from Rosland Island. They did come down one more time; it's been two years since I saw them. I'm looking forward to seeing everyone.

We reviewed the next leg of our trip, before we all called it a night. We are going to stop at the four corners. Four corners are where four states connect together, which are: New Mexico, Arizona, Utah, and Colorado. Then we are going to go to Cortez, Colorado. There are Indian ruins that we wanted to check out. Mesa Verde is the main one that we wanted to see. We have friends there, and they had told us all about the area. It sounds like it has quite the history. They also own the only campground in town. Looks like everyone settled in for the night. Well another day gone, time to call it a day!

CHAPTER 6

Day 3
NM, CO

It's hard to believe we have only been on the road three days. We are getting faster about breaking down. During breakfast we talked about Maria and James leaving us in Albuquerque, NM. James wanted to visit his family in Fountain, it is outside of Colorado Springs, and spends a couple of days with them.

We will meet up in Green River, UT with Maria and family. Maria is a lot like me, she likes keeping a journal of her adventures. I asked her, can I get a copy of it I want to add it to my journal. She agreed, it would be a good idea, and joked maybe we'll write a book! You never know I told her. We're going to miss them, but I understand James hasn't seen his family for three years. I hope they have a great time.

We moved people around this time, I was riding with Wanda and the Frank's were driving the RV. Twila and Dennis were bringing up the rear. All of the kids wanted to ride in the RV; the Frank's weren't too sure about it. But Daniel and Tina said, "They would keep them in line." Douglas asked if he could ride in the lead vehicle with us. I told him sure, you can be the navigator, and I'll sit in the back and enjoy the ride. Everyone was settled in to their vehicles and we headed out to the next adventure! Maria and James were following behind Twila, because it wasn't too far to their turn off, it's about 118 miles. Our next campsite is Cortez, CO, which is about 400 miles, highway 40, and then Hwy 666 up to Shiprock, which has a rock that looks like a ship out in the desert. Then a stop at the four corners, which should put us in Cortez around early evening.

We're driving through the Laguna and Ramah-Navajo Indian reservation. The towns we have seen from the road are small and we saw one Indian village on top of a hill. It looked like it was still being used. It was built out of mud bricks, like the Indian ruins that we had seen before. It's nice riding in the back; I can write in my journal and enjoy the views as we go.

Looks like we're going to stop outside of Gallup and have lunch, there is a nice rest area on top of the hill, so we can see the whole valley. Guess it's time to stop writing and get everyone some lunch.

What a view, we had sandwiches, pork beans and chips for lunch, and enjoyed the air and view. Next stop four corners, and then Cortez, which is only 138 miles.

Wow! What a day, we stopped at four corners, there isn't much there. There is a marker that shows where the states meet and some Ute Indian selling necklaces and other things. Of course, we all had to stand in each state, not every day you can be in four states in five minutes. The campground our friends own is really nice; they have an area for family travelers. What I mean by that is we put the trailers in a circle and there is a big fire pit for us to use. They have already planned dinner for us, we had steak and hog dogs with pinto beans and salad on the side. We had met Judy and Fred when Frank was in the army. Judy was in the army and Fred worked for Civilian Services. They have three kids, two boys and one girl. Their kids have their own band, so we had live music after dinner. They played country and some 60's. It was great fun; we haven't danced that much in a long time! We did a lot of things with Judy's family back then. They liked the same things we did; we did a lot of camping and hiking with them. We use to go out to the clubs with them and dance up a storm.

Fred is from this area, and knows where the best places to go are. As we sat around the camp fire, Fred told us about how he found out about all of the Indian ruins in this area.

Fred's story: One summer we were visiting our Aunt and Uncle at their home in Dove Creek, Colorado. Every day that we were there, we took a drive out to different Indians ruin sites and looked at the local attractions.

One day we planned to visit Mesa Verde National Park near Mancos and Cortez, Colorado. The main attraction there is a series of rock dwellings that have been built into the cliff face. They have names such as Cliff Palace, Spruce Tree House, and others. They had little pathways that ran down near the structures. We were close enough to get a good look inside of them. Or you could peer over the edge of the Kiva. It is a round structure, built into the ground, used by Shaman as a holy place.

On the rim above Cliff Palace, there was a visitor center that you could look at the different exhibits of items found during excavation. That way it helped you learn a little bit more about the people that the Archeologists, determined that they were the builders of the Cliff drawings. They called them the Anasazi, which is what the local modern-day Navajo Indians called them. The word meant "Ancient ones."

Besides the regular exhibits of: woven baskets, footwear, and the usual things that you would expect in a museum. There was a glass case, in the center of the exhibit room which was the star exhibit. It was the mummified remains of an Anasazi woman, they called her Esther. She was completely intact, her hair, skin, everything! She was sitting with her legs drawn up to her chest. She had a painful expression on her face and was sticking her tongue out, and it was stuck over her upper lip. Her dark skin was covered in wrinkles, and had the appearance of tanned leather.

Because of the expression on her face, it was thought that she may have died in childbirth. They had determined that she must have lived about 800 years ago, when life in the Cliff dwelling was a bustling place, but now is the ruins of Mesa Verde.

The kids were listening to every word Fred said. The mummy got the grandkids attention the most; they wanted to go see it. But Fred told them, she has been removed, because the Native Indian didn't want their ancestry to be put on display like that. He wasn't sure what had happened to her. He ensured the kids, there were lots to see, and maybe they will even find some arrow heads.

Our kids and theirs were having a good time catching up on everything too. The grandkids were doing marshmallow on a stick. Of course, they had to see how many they could get on a stick without burning them. I guess the record is five, and Douglas is the winner.

As the evening wore on, Judy, our friend told us about the things they had planned for us tomorrow, it sounded like a full day. She told us we needed to get to Mesa Verde early, so we can watch the sunrise on the mountain. It lights up the village, and the yellow and red stones are beautiful. It sounds wonderful, I guess it's time to call it another day.

CHAPTER 7

Day 4
Cortez, CO

What a great day, when Judy said earlier, that there was a lot of walking, and how beautiful it was there, she wasn't kidding. We got up at 5 and she had breakfast already going. There was bacon, sausage, pancakes, eggs and cereal for the kids. What a great breakfast. Judy reminded everyone to wear hiking boots; we'll be doing a lot of walking. We packed our lunch in our back packs, and filled our canteens. We had to take five cars; there were a lot of us, between our family and theirs.

We arrived in time to see the sunrise onto the Cliff dwelling, it was amazing. You could imagine seeing people walking around doing their daily tasks; getting the fire started, going for water, getting ready for the day and all the things they had to do to get ready for the next day. It reminded me of how Frank and I had lived on Rosland Island.

Fred was our tour guide he was great, we had a lot of questions and he had all the answers for us. One thing I really like about Fred, he likes to know the history of everything. The first place we stopped at was the "Cliff Palace" it was built inside an alcove. The Cliff houses were made out of sandstone. Sandstone is a very porous material; it was easy to carve out the building. Well it was easier than other stones or mud bricks.

It was hard to believe hundreds of people lived in this area at one time. "The majority of alcoves within Mesa Verde are small crevices or ledges able to have room for only a few small rooms. Most were too small for larger building." According to our guide, "The cliff dwelling was first discovered in 1888 by some ranchers." I couldn't even imagine finding something like this. We walked along a small path, and every ruin we came to have another story to tell. Some of the names of the different ruins are: Cliff Palace, Balcony House, Spruce Tree House, Long House, Step House and Wetherill. Each had a story to go with it, way too many to write in my journal. I did take a lot of pictures today. We stopped and had lunch at the museum.

Then we headed off to Long house, which was about 12 miles from where we were. It was a dusty road, so we had to go slow, so we didn't cover everyone behind us with dust. It was the longest 12 miles I think I have ever gone on. Anyway, there is a reason it was called Long House. It is a long house built inside another alcove, and it was one long wall that looked like a house, it had a couple of opening. One of the things I found interesting is they had these things called Kiva which are round.

Inside of them it remained 50 degrees all year round, in the summer it was cool and in the winter they just built a little fire.

There was a few hiking trails, one was two miles round trip; we had lots of water, so we decide to take it. All the grandkids needed to be let loose and have some fun. Of course, we told them what to watch out for and not to pick up any creatures along the way. I was amazed how many creatures live in the desert. There are all kinds of different types of lizards. There is one here called a Mountain Boomer, it is bright blue, with little yellow spots on its top and have an orange chest, some were just brown. Then there were Whiptails, and horned lizards. The kids had fun chasing them and every once in awhile they would catch one. The younger kids wanted to pet them, the older grandkids would hold them so they could. The little grandkids had to be carried on the way back. The guys just put them on their shoulders; of course they had to have a race to the cars, the last 20 feet. It was funny to see five grown men with kids on their shoulders running though the desert, with teenagers chasing after them.

After we got back we cleaned up, I was so happy they had restrooms with showers. Judy and her family said they would be back after they get cleaned up too. The plan for dinner tonight is a big pot of stew, which has been cooking all day. Judy said she will bring the corn bread. Well I need to get things ready for dinner.

It was going to be a little bit before dinner, when I heard Wanda say, "See you; I'm going to do some laundry." She was taking her youngest son Douglas with her. When they got back Wanda and Douglas had a story to tell us. According to what I heard later.

Wanda was sorting the clothes into the washers. She was checking the pockets of the jeans, when she found something squishy. She let out ayah! A salamander fell onto the floor. She hollered at Douglas to get it quick. The salamander was headed under the washer. Douglas grabbed it by the tail and of course the tail came off, it made it under the washer. Douglas got down on his hands and knees to try to see it. Wanda asked, if he could see it. He said "No mom, I wonder where it went. It was a good size one too." They went over to the bench next to the wall, while they waited for the wash to be done. They kept looking around to see if they could spot it.

Finally the wash was done and the clothes were put into the dryer. So far no one had come into the building. Later when the clothes were done and they were loading the baskets, Wanda decided not to fold them. Douglas asked her how come you're not folding the clothes. Wanda replied "No need, we will fold them in the trailer; I just want to get out of here." Just then a young tall lady came in with a basket of clothes. She was dressed like she was going to a party. Wanda told Doug, "Come on honey." As they were rushing out, the woman threw down her basket of clothes and went screaming out the door, her high heels clicking across the floor.

As Wanda and Douglas looked behind them the lady was headed to the Main office. When they got back to their camping spot they told the others what happened. They just laughed. Later when they were pulling out to leave they saw a security guard. He was standing by the entrance to the office. He was showing some people the salamander, which he called a "Mountain Boomer" that he had in a net. They were laughing, poor little tailless thing. Douglas told his Mom, "That's my

Salamander!" Wanda said "Don't worry about it, you can find another one."

The rest of the evening was great, the beef stew had all kinds of favor; I guess they put pinto beans in everything they cook here. The cornbread was great too. Afterwards we sat around the fire and sang songs and told ghost stories. We talked about where we were going tomorrow, Fred said, "We'll have to drive a little farther but the area is less known to the tourists and the kids can run around and enjoy themselves. Funny how vacation can be so much work, but so far it has been great. One place we are going to is called "Hovenweep," which means "Deserted valley." Then we will be going to ruins called Square Tower Group. I guess we'll find out tomorrow, it's been a long day, time to call it a night.

CHAPTER 8

Day 5
Cortez, CO area

It was nice to sleep in, I started hearing people moving around about 7 am, but Frank and I just laid there enjoying the time alone, well kind of alone. Then we heard Twila yelling "Get up you lazy heads, we're burning day light!" I turned to Frank and said, I wonder where she gets that from, as usual he just smiled and gave me a little push and asked well what are you waiting for?

What a great way to start off the morning, the coffee was made and breakfast was on the table. Fred and Judy were by themselves this time; their kids had to go to work today. We got ready for the trip, lots of water and a picnic lunch and snacks. We only took two cars this time.

We started at a few smaller ruins that most tourists don't know about. It was great, we could go inside and the kids had a great time finding pottery and even found a few arrowheads by the creek area. Then we headed to Hovenweep. Fred said, "It was used as a lookout of Ancestral Puebloan ruins in a background of sage and juniper. The village was abandoned around the late 1200s. It was interesting how the ancient buildings were positioned on the edges of the cliffs, balanced over boulder heaps, or guarding seeps." Frank asked Fred what is a seeps? Fred said "It is a moist or wet place where water can be found, it is usually a small pool of water, which comes from underground aquifer.

Next we hiked to the Square Tower House and Hovenweep Castle. According to Fred, "There were portals in the castle that appeared to align with the sunlight each seasonal solstice and equinox. Hovenweep is both a mystical pilgrimage and a fascinating study in ancient culture." I was surprised about the different features of the Hovenweep ruins. They are amazing towers-square, oval, circles, and D shaped buildings. There were ruins of buildings everywhere. The Anasazi Indians sure like to build; I could only imagine how many mud bricks they had to build and the time it took to do all this. It's a wonder how it is all still here. It is hard to in vision the village hard at work, kids playing like our kids are doing now.

They had a nice picnic area; we found a table under one of the biggest trees in the area. Juniper trees don't really get that big, but big enough to give us a little shade. We handed out sandwiches, chips and then had the kids drink some water before they took off down to the creek, to see what else they could find.

We were just sitting at the table when we heard Sharlene screaming and calling for us to come see what Douglas had. We ran down the hill and there was Douglas holding a stick with a skull at the end of it. He was chasing them around with it. Frankie yelled at him to stop it, and Douglas turned to his dad, and had a big grin on his face with an expression of what! Frankie asked him "where did you find that?" Douglas pointed over to a small cave that they had found. Douglas said, "There was even more bones inside!" Fred told Frankie that Douglas needs to put the skull back where he found it. Douglas wanted to keep it, but they explained to him that it wasn't the right thing to do. He agreed so he crawled back into the hole and put the skull back where he found it. Douglas suggested that we should fill the entryway with rocks, so no one else will find them. "Good idea," Fred said.

It didn't take long to pile up rocks up in front of the hole; we even threw a little bit of dirt on it to make it look like it's been there a while. I told the kids to go down and wash their hands in the creek. Judy suggested that we hike over to the other side of the Valley to see what was there. We headed up the other side of the Valley. When we arrived at the top of the Valley it was a surprise, it was amazing. There were more ruins, not as big as the others on the opposite side. But you could tell that there was a village there at one time. The rest of the day went without incident. We all had a great time looking at all of the desert plants and animals that we found. I must be getting old, my legs are killing me tonight from all the walking we done the last two days. But we will be heading out tomorrow to Utah.

After we got cleaned up, we decided to go to the bowling alley and have dinner and let the kids bowl. We had a couple pitchers of beer and watched everyone enjoying the evening together. It was nice to relax and not have to worry about cooking dinner and having a couple beers with good friends is always a nice evening. Judy asked us "Where was our next stop, I told her we were going to stay a couple of days in Moab, UT and then meet Maria in Green River, then head to my folks home in Salina. To our surprise Judy asked us, if we would like some company. Fred and she really didn't have much to do for the rest of this week and they haven't been to Moab in a long time. We said that would be great, we plan on leaving around 8. Fred said, "Great, we'll be ready. After awhile we called it a night, the grandkids were getting pretty tired. Sharlene had already fallen asleep on a chair, she looked so cute. Dennis picked her up, and she didn't make a sound. Nice thing is the RV Park was right across the street from the bowling alley. Well another day is gone; it's time to go to sleep.

CHAPTER 9

Moab, UT
Day 6

Were not traveling very far today, Fred said he has a friend that has a really nice campground we can stay at, his going to take the lead. It's my turn to drive the RV; this will be my first time. Hopefully everything goes well. We had a light breakfast before we headed out. We're all getting really good at breaking down and even faster setting up. Even the little ones have jobs to do. When we fixed our own meals for the crew, us gals figured a way to share the chores. There were four of us so we teamed up two and two. We got things done in no time at all. We always were in a hurry to get on with our adventure.

Another wonderful day, I didn't do too badly on driving the RV. I didn't think the roads was that small, but when you're driving a RV, they get really small. Frank was really good about not yelling at me. But I could tell by how white his hands were, he was holding on for dear life. Most of the way there was a two lane highways, but we knew of a short cut, so we took it. It ended up taking more time, because a farmer had to move his cattle from one range to another. The problem was the trail just happened to be our shortcut. One thing you never do is hurry cattle or blow your horn. After about an hour of following the cattle, we came to a turn off so we ended back on the highway. At least we had a bathroom and food for the kids in the RV. We finally arrived in Moab, as we pulled into the camp ground, I hit a pole, because of what I saw, and otherwise I did great.

As I pulled into the campground I saw my folks, Grace and Lazelle (aka Mom and Dad). Even my brother Darren and my sister Jill and their kids were there. They all had big smiles on their faces. As soon as I stopped the RV, they ran over and yelled "Surprise!" I turned and looked at everyone in our RV and they were all smiling. It dawned on me why all the grandkids wanted to ride with us. Everyone knew they would be here except me. I found out later Judy and Fred had worked it all out with the others and Frank. It was a wonderful surprise. Today is my birthday, I'm 63 today. What a great family, they had cake and everything else already set up!

Jill is my older sister, and she looks ten years younger than me. She still lives in Delta City, with her three kids, two boys and one girl. It's been about three years since we saw them last. What great looking kids! Jill's husband died in the Vietnam War, he was in the Navy, and was killed in action. She is a teacher at our old high school; she teaches English and P.E., the kids just love her. Her kids look so much like her. She told me she had a surprise for me when we get back to Delta City. I tried to get it out of her, but no luck.

Darren is the youngest of us and he looks just like our Dad. For that matter so does Jill. Both have dark black hair and dark skin. Me I take after Mom, light brown hair and as white as can be. Well I would be if it wasn't for the tan, I usually have! Anyway Darren met his wife Enola her freshman year of high school. According to Enola he didn't have a chance; she knew he would someday be her husband. They have three boys; all grown up and are so handsome and great kids.

Darren has always had a dream of owning his own business, but he wanted it to be something that would help people. When Darren set his mind to something he does it. He made his dream come true. He owns a company that helps people in the sports world; it helps them train better and shows them what to work on to make improvement on their training and development. Enola is the VP and runs the office and deals with the day to day things. Maria named her daughter after Enola, because Enola used to have her come up and visit when she was younger. They are very close to each other. While we were missing, Enola came down to help where ever she could.

We spent most of today setting up camp; we had one whole end of the campground for just our group. The view was amazing, you could see for miles and the red rocks mountain range was beautiful. They fixed up the rec. center for my birthday. As I walked over to my parent's trailer, I could smell it. It was my favorite dish my mom makes "Spanish Beans." What a great day!

I love this part of Utah; Moab it originally was used to serve as the Colorado River crossing during the 1800. There is a lot of history here, it once had a fort but was abandoned in the late 1800. As I noted earlier the Colorado River isn't too far from Moab. I guess you could say it's a hop, skip and jump from where we are camping. We all went on a boat ride down the Colorado River to watch the sunset and to enjoy the cool air from the river. There is so much wild life along the river and there are rocks that have a shape of a rabbit, another of a frog, and many more. When we got back we had a camp fire and roasted some marshmallows. The kids were hungry again, so we cooked some hog dogs too. My Dad loves to tell stories about the history of Utah. He told the kids how the soldiers used to protect the area. In the long run the Indians won out, until 1902 when the settlers came back, and took over the land. I keep asking him to write down his stories so I would have them. But that still hasn't happened.

As the night wore on, the grandkids started falling asleep, so it ended up with the adults that didn't have kids to take care of. We had two picnic tables and we had two different games going, Aggravation and Pinochle. If you lose you had to move to the next table. The winner had a choice if they wanted to move or not to the other table. I explained to everyone it is my birthday so I should always win. No one agreed with me, go figure! You could hear the crickets in the distance other than that it was quite, except for us of course.

Tomorrows plan is to take the boat down the river again. We wanted to show the kids the Indian writing on the walls of the canyon and show them the dinosaur foot prints. Then we'll be heading up to see the Hole N" the Rock, the Arches National Park, and the Canyon lands. It's going to be another full day. Fred and Judy will be heading home in the morning; they got a call from their kid and needed to leave. One of the grandkids had gotten ill and wasn't doing too well.

We promised to see each other more often. We told them they needed to come to Houston and we could take the boat out and do some fishing. Fred really liked that idea! It is time to get some sleep we have a long day ahead of us tomorrow.

CHAPTER 10

Moab, UT
Day 7

I t was nice to sit around the camp fire this morning. I
wasn't the first one up; the grandkids always are up
first. My Mom and Dad were up too. Dad always said,
"You're wasting the day, if you're not up by 5:00. I had another
bowl of Spanish beans for breakfast; I could eat it three times
a day. After awhile Mom and Dad couldn't stand it anymore
and they went from trailer to trailer (our family only) telling
everyone to get up, "We're burning day light!" My parents are in
their late 70's and they act like there in their earlier 60s.

It didn't take long before everyone started coming out of
their trailers and tents. What a group, there was over twenty
of us now. Darren and Jill didn't bring their better half, they
couldn't get off work. There was a lot of hugging to go around

and we talked about what we were going to do today. Canteens were filled and sandwiches made. We filled up the backpacks, and loaded up the cars.

First stop the Hole N" Rock, this is an amazing place, we used to come here and visit the Christensen family, and they had a little café inside the rock. They ended up with 14 rooms, and excavated 50,000 cubic feet of sandstone from the rock to build their home. Our kids saw it when they were little, but haven't seen it in a long time. It is interesting that Mr. Christensen and his brother used the small alcove for camping; they would sleep inside the alcove at night. I guess somewhere in his mind he knew it was home. It was fun seeing our kids and grandkids seeing what I saw as a little girl. Even being an older woman now, I am still in wonderment of the work he and his wife did. We went on the tour which really didn't take that long, about fifteen minutes. The guys had a lot of questions, and our group was all family, so it was no big deal.

Next we went to the Arches, the road is long and narrow but the view like everywhere else in Utah is beautiful. After a long day it was nice to get back to camp. Tomorrow we will be heading to Green River to join up with Maria and her family. It's only been a couple of days, but I miss them. We normally see or talk to each other every day. I think we're trying to make up for lost time.

After seeing my family, I was surprise to see how much our kids look like them. Maria is a lot like her Grandma Grace, you can see the Indian in her, and she has long black hair. She has to fight with her weigh all the time. She is the shortest one in the family; she is only 5' 4". She has a big heart and she is the smartest one of the kids. Twila takes after my father's side, she

54

is tall and has long blond-brown hair, she is also taller than me; she is 5' 10". She is hard headed and likes to be in control, but she also has a big heart, and takes in all kinds of animals.

Which drives Dennis crazy, but he is right there to help her out when needed. If you look at a picture of my sister Jill and Twila next to each other, you would swear it was the same person. Now Frankie, he is just like his Dad and his side of the family. He has dark hair, and tall like his Dad, and slim. He could eat cake every day, and never gain a pound.

CHAPTER 11

Day 8
Green River, UT

It didn't take us long to get from Moab to Green River. So after we set up camp we went to the river to do some fishing. Luckily, it was a good time to go, there were six of us, and we caught 10 fish. We're having a fish fry tonight. We paid for Maria's camping spot, we didn't want the camp ground to fill up, because then she wouldn't have anywhere to park. It filled up pretty quick, after we arrived here; we arrived a little after 2 pm. We had the kids make a "Welcome back sign for Maria and her family. We hung it up in their space. They arrived just in time for dinner, there were hugs all around.

After Maria added her last day into her journal, she gave it to me so I could add it to my journal later. It looks like they had a great time. We sat around the campfire and talked about what we have been up to and James was telling us all about his family, and how great it was to spend time with them.

Maria Journal

We left my family today, their headed to Cortez, CO and we're headed to Fountain, CO, where James family lives. We wanted to go visit with James family, while we were in the area. Well kind of! We ended up at James's folk's home around 7:00pm. Everyone was waiting for us. There were his parents, his four sister and two brothers. I couldn't count all of the cousins, niece and nephews.

Our girls were excited to see their cousins; most of them were around their age. Being little girls there was a lot of screaming in the beginning. Enola and Treva wanted to show them our trailer and all the rocks they have collected so far. I had to stop them twice, I told them to wait until tomorrow. I needed to clean it up before anyone went inside.

James looked so happy to see everyone. Everyone was talking all at once, I'm really not sure if anyone was listening, but it sure looked like they were having a great time. I couldn't image not seeing my family on a regular basis. James hasn't seen his family in two years. His parents came down for a couple of weeks, about a year ago. His brother and sister haven't been to see us, between their jobs and money it never worked out. But we did write each other and send pictures. Once a month James would call his folks house, on a Sunday, his brother and sister would be there to get in a few words too.

They had already planned for tomorrow, we will be going to the lake and do some fishing, boating and hiking. James families are very much outdoor people. They go hunting as often as they can, and will pretty much hunt for anything that is legal to hunt. We didn't get to bed until late, but it was great fun meeting all of James relatives, the kids have grown a lot. I met the addition to the family, husbands and babies alike. Well it is time to call it a night.

Day 2

We got up early to go fishing; I never got up this early on a regular day. I'm beginning to wonder about vacations. James family decided to have a fishing contest today. By noon I was ahead, I had caught four fish, but then after a little while James took the lead. For the rest of the day, it went back and forth. The fishing contest included anything you caught in the water, which could have been: crawfish, eels, frogs and so on. The girls had a great time Enola caught one fish and Treva caught two fish and one frog. James told Treva that, "Its legs will be good eating." She told him no, and put it back into the water.

By the time we headed home James was ahead, so he won the contest. I told him I let him win. Funny thing is they didn't tell us what you would win, until after James won. He won the right to clean all of the fish. All together we ended up catching 20 fish, one eel (which was too small to eat) and a basket of crawfish. The fish weighted from 5lbs to 8 lbs. Good thing we have enough people to eat them all.

We had a great time at the lake, James brother had a party boat (that's what I'm going to call it). He built it himself, you can BBQ on it and there is a slide that is at the end of the boat. It is a great boat for swimming, sunbathing and partying. They like their lakes as much as we like our oceans.

We had a picnic and hike around the lake, well not completely around the lake, James brother picked us up at the dock on the other side. It was a beautiful place to spend the day, the pine trees were huge and everything was so green.

When we got back to James folk's place, we cleaned the fish, and then threw the guts into the pond for the fish and turtle to eat. It was amazing the way the fish and turtle went after it. James's Dad took charge of the cooking. His mom had already made the potatoes and macaroni salad. She even had the corn on the cob ready to put on the BBQ, and tons of other things. She does love to cook, I guess raising seven kids you would have to. James's Dad cooked the fish a couple different ways. He cooked them in a pan, which had some kind of sauce. Then straight on the grill and some in aluminum foil. Needles to say I tried each type. I couldn't believe how much I ate.

James parents live out in the country, they have about twenty acres, and it has a pond, a shop and a really nice house. One part of their property is set up like a park, with a swing set and a fire pit. They even have power going out to it, so if you want to park a trailer out there you can. That's where our trailer is parked at now. From my understanding the kids will bring their trailers out during the summer and hang out there. For now, we have our own private camp ground!

Of course, the girls reminded me that I said it was ok for them to have visitor in our trailer. One nice thing, it really doesn't take much to clean it up. The girls asked if their cousins could spend the night, we couldn't come up with a reason to say no, so we said yes. James sister said, she would take the girls tomorrow night, they wanted to have all of the cousins come over for a sleep over. Sounds like fun, I'm glad I'm not the one doing it. This will be the first night we will have our trailer alone, Happy Night!

Day 3

What a busy day, after breakfast we all loaded up and went up to Pike Peak, what a view, the road was a little scary other than that it was pretty cool. Then we went to the Garden of the Gods, we hiked around there and had lunch. What a beautiful place, I can see why they called it the Garden of the Gods, it was so colorful.

We ended up at James sister's house; they live in a small town not too far from the Gardens. We helped get things set up for the cousins party (just the kids), the teenagers offered to help with the younger ones. Around nine o'clock we headed back to James's parents place. Tomorrow we head back to join my family. I can't help thinking; I can't wait to get back to my family. I know Enola and Treva are ready to get back to my family. We are having a great time, especially James. He really needed to get together with his family. I know the girls were anxious to hear more of mom's stories about when mom and dad were stranded on the island. They kept telling their cousins about my parent's stories, about all the things they discovered. The girls wanted to hear all about the merbeings, aka mermaids. Every time one of the girls would call them mermaids, Enola would correct them.

Day 4

What a great night last night, it was so nice having the place to ourselves. They didn't bring the girls back until 9 am, so we just lay in bed enjoying the morning. We joined James parents for coffee and breakfast, that's when the girls showed up. We had said our good bye to everyone yesterday; we were on the road by 10. Next stop Green River, UT.

I've been thinking I can't wait to get back to the others. I know Enola and Treva are ready to join back up with my family. We did have a good time, especially James. He really needed to get together with his family. I know the girls were anxious to hear more of Mom's stories about when Mom and Dad were stranded on the island. Even thou they had heard the stories many times.

We arrived in Green River around 5 p.m. and my family was already there. I was surprised to see Grandpa Lazelle, Grandma Grace, my Uncle Darren and Aunt Jill and their kids. What a great surprise, they even had a space saved for us. With a welcome back sign! I gave mom my journal, I hope she enjoys it! THE END

It was a great night; it is good to have Maria and her family back. The whole time, we talked about how much Maria or one of her family would love this or that. We did collect rocks for Enola and Treva for their collection. They couldn't stop talking about the rocks, they picked up at James folk's place, or the ones we gave them. Their collections should be pretty big by the time we get home. Grandpa and James already said they would build them a keepsake box for each of the grandkids.

The fish were great; James's Dad gave them some of the special sauce he made for fish. Of course we had to try it, it was awesome! The guys and some of the grandkids wanted to do some night fishing. When they came back, they had another 10 fish. They cleaned the fish and put them in the ice chest. We'll cook them at my folk's place tomorrow or the next day. I think we could eat fish every day, oh yea we did!

Our next stop is my parents place; they live outside of Delta City. It's a nice place to grow up. There weren't many jobs in the area, but the ranch we had paid the bills and kept food on the table. Later on they found beryllium, it is refined outside town. They grow alfalfa and as Dad would say "Fossils and Mineral, for the tourist to come dig for." Most of the fossils are Trilobite. Topaz, obsidian, opal and geodes are what people come looking for. It has changed a lot since I grew up there.

Well everyone is settling in for the night. I guess I need to get some sleep. We won't have to get up so early, it won't take long to get to Delta City from Green River.

CHAPTER 12

Day 9
Delta City, UT my hometown

We arrived in Delta City about noon, Mom and Dad had already set up a place for us all to set up our rigs and camp on their property. They have 300 acres, right on the boarder of the Gunnison Bend Reservoir. My great grandpa lost 400 acres when they put in the reservoir. From what he told me, it wasn't a big loss, it was just desert anyway.

My brother Darren and my sister Jill families were there to meet us. Darren has three boys and Jill has two boys and one girl. Again hugs all around and kids talking a mile a minute. It was wonderful to see everyone! Their kids have grown so much. I need to put rocks on their head to keep them from growing, as Mom used to tell us.

I need to add a little history about Delta City. It began in 1907, but before that it was called Burtner. This is where they relocated thousands of Japanese-Americans and put them in internment camps, they told the locals that it was to protect military installations from espionage. The local's didn't have a say one way or the other about the camp.

After we had lunch, the grandkids, well all of us wanted to go dig for fossils and minerals. My folks of course knew where the best places were. It was great fun, every time someone found something, everyone would have to run over and check it out. It was fun to watch after they found a fossil. They would carry it over to the table where Sharlene and Tina were in charge of, keeping everything organized. They are our little organizers. They would put the name of the person on it, and then at the end of the day we would have a contest. There would be one for the best fossil and one for the best mineral. We found a lot of geodes, my Dad told the kids he would cut them when we get back to the farm. You never knew they had something inside; they just look like regular rocks, except they are round.

I was sitting under the tent, when I notice Daniel and Douglas was missing. I asked Frankie, where his boys were? He pointed and said, "They went over there." Then I saw the boys coming over the hill, and they were carrying a big rock. They both had big smiles on their faces. I yelled what did you find? They yelled back, "Something really cool!" Everyone stopped doing what they were doing. All the other kids ran over to see what they had. They took it over to my Dad; he was the man in the know!

As he looked at it, all he could say was "I'll be damn! I have no clue what it is. I guess we'll have to pull the fossil book out when we get home. Guess who won the contest for the best fossil.

Frankie and Dad wanted the boys to show them where they found the fossil. After awhile they came back and had a couple of more fossils, which were Trilobite. These were much bigger than the ones we were finding where we were digging. Everyone wanted to go over to the new site but it was getting late, so we headed back to the house.

After dinner, Dad told everyone to bring their geodes to the barn and he would cut them. It was fun to watch the kids' expression when Grandpa would hand them their geode back. Each were different, the colors were amazing. We lined up all of the geodes to see all the different types. No two are the same. The main colors were blue, red, dirt yellow and white. Geodes are solid inside, but every once in awhile you will find one that doesn't follow the rules. One of Enola geodes that she had found was one of them that didn't follow the rules. It had clear crystal in it, with black spots, and when the sunlight hit it, its brilliant reflection was incredible.

We ended up having the fish the guys caught out of the Green River yesterday. They were great! My Dad has his own way of cooking his fish. He coats them with cracker and bread crumbs with seasoning in the mix. They are to wonderful, a nice change. We also had pork ribs and all the "fixens" to go with them, as Mom would say.

As the evening went on, people started showing up. There was friends and family, even some of my high school friends. I kept in touch with about a half dozen of them. All of them had questions about when Frank and I were stranded on Rosland Island. I began to feel like a celebrity. We talked about the good old days in high school and the things we used to do. Both of my folks were shaking their heads and Frank had a big smile on his face. Our kids kept asking my high school friends about different things. I put a stop to that after a little while.

As I looked at my friends I couldn't help but think how old everyone looked. If I have to say so myself I think I am the youngest looking one in the group! Well Frank told me that too! Most have never left this area; few had left but ended up returning. They liked the slow pace of the area and all the different things you can do here. Funny part is that is the way Frank and I feel about being on the ocean. Tomorrow we are going up to the mountain to find the area I saw in the dream room on Rosland Island.

When I was in the dream room on the Rosland Island, there was a cliff which was overlooking a large valley, and it was all red stones and as the sun hit the walls of the Valley, it looked like it was on fire. It was as gorgeous as I remembered it from when I was a child. I could see the eagles flying overhead and herds of elk down in the Valley. As I stood on top of the cliff I could hear the calls of the different animals.

The elk were singing and yelling at another herd farther down in the Valley and they were responding back. The eagles were also screaming, and enjoying the airflow in the Valley. It was a gorgeous day there was a light breeze. As I wandered along the edge of the cliff I saw a herd of deer, and some cattle in a field. I could even see an old homestead in the distance, with smoke coming out of the chimney. This is so real it's kind of scary, but as I stood there I could feel myself being a part of the scene instead of just watching.

I found a path going down the cliff side and decided to take it. As I walked down the path I continued to watch the action in the valley below. The path looked like it was made by the animals that lived here, and it was used a lot. It was easy to travel down, as I got closer to the different herds, there were horses, elk, deer and cattle, but they all seem to move away, as I got closer. They continued to move around and to speak to each other, and then all of a sudden I was back in the room with Frank.

Tomorrow we will go find this place, I saw in the dream room. I can't wait to see it again.

Day 10
Visited my dream spot!

We found the area I saw in the dream room. It was more beautiful than I remembered. Everyone was amazed how accurate I had described it. Even the little farmhouse with the smoke coming out of the chimney was there. Sharlene was so excited she went looking for the path I had talked about and she found it. She called to me, "Come on Grandma let's go see where it goes. Everyone started heading toward the path. Sharlene put her hand up and said, "Grandma first!" They all said at once, "Yes Ma'am!" I walked to the front of the line and took Sharlene's hand. I felt like a queen!

As we hiked down the mountain side, we could hear the elk calling to each other and the eagles screaming at each other. It was almost noon, we arrived just in time to see the sun hit the canyon walls; it looked like they were on fire. The canyon walls had orange and red walls, which glowed when the sun hit them. I felt like there was no other place on earth like this. As we got to the end of the path there was a creek that fed into a medium size pond. We could see livestock and wildlife drinking water; some were lying under the trees. The young ones were playing with each other in the field. They acted like they didn't care if we were there or not. They felt no danger from us. Which was a surprise, you'll have to remember there was a lot of us, sixteen! But you wouldn't know it, because everyone was so quite. We stood there and watched for awhile, and then we headed back up the cliff.

There was energy in that valley, everything was in harmony. Accept for the one little cabin, there was no other humans in this valley, accept of course us. We were welcome, but not invited to stay, if that makes any sense to you.

As we stood at the top of the cliff, we all stood there in silence enjoying the magnificence view we had found. I think all of us hated the idea of leaving but it was time to go. The road we had to travel on wasn't very wide, I was hoping the whole time we wouldn't run into anyone going either way. We were lucky no cars. There is no way I would have taken the Seamore up here!

We stopped in Delta City on our way back, we wanted to do some shopping and see if anything has changed. We drove by my old school and the restaurant I used to work at as a teenager. We stopped in and had a late lunch; the owner was the son of the man I had worked for when I was in High School. Small world! Well small city! After lunch we went and visited the Great Basin Museum. For being a small town, there have been a lot of things that has happen here, from floods to internment of Japanese-American people.

There are so many memories here, when I was old enough I worked at the small café, downtown. But most summer we worked on my folk's ranch. During haying season, our cousins and friends would help with the haying. We would get up early before the sun was up, have breakfast and then out to the fields. We would work all day until it was too dark to see the bales. It was hard work but we made it into games. We would have contest on who could load their truck up the fastest. Or we would roll the hay bales down the hill, and the first one down the hill, didn't have to work for fifteen minutes.

One time, one of my smaller cousins was trying to help and he was pushing a bale over, and some how he got caught in the bale so he rolled over the bale and he rolled over it. It was the funniest thing to see. He didn't get hurt, but he didn't want to help anymore.

One thing about living on a farm you worked hard to keep it running, but there are so many things to do. We uses to go fishing at the pond, I would put three lines out and wait for a fish to bite, then I would put it in a bucket of water. I hated killing them; I discover early on, that if I held the pole I wouldn't get a bite. But if I just set the poles up by themselves I would catch fish. We had a lot of catfish in the pond. The neighbor down the road raised them, but the water supply to his pond ran out. He asked Dad if he wanted them, and he said sure, and sent us kids to go catch them. We learned really fast about the spikes they had on each side of their head. We ended up with three burlap bags of them. We took them to our pond and dumb them in. Not one of them died, within a year they double in the amount we had caught earlier.

Of course, we had horses! We had lots of room to ride, and we would ride out to the forest area and camp out. We would tell ghost stories and try to scare each other. Dad and Mom would go to the auction and buy the old horses no one wanted and let them run free on our land. It was pretty cool to see a herd of horse running free.

We got back from our day and settled in for a BBQ at my folks place and enjoyed the evening. We're going to stay here for another day and then head out to Austin, NV. We're just going to hang around the farm and enjoy the time with our family and friends.

As we were sitting around the fire, little David was cooking a marshmallow and it caught on fire and he started swing it back and forth. When all of sudden it flew off and hit Sue's jeans. It caught her jeans on fired. Next thing you know Doug jumps up and puts her on the ground and threw dirt on it and put out the fire. It all happened so fast, after it was over with, we all started cheering. Sue gave Doug a big hug and thanked him. Then we went back to talking about when we grew up and the things we did. Like nothing ever happened.

It was a great place to grow up. Of course, my parents played a big part in making it a great place. No matter what work we had to do, we would find a way to make it fun.

Day 11
Just relaxing at home

First thing in the morning Jill came over and said let's go. I asked her where and she said "It's time for you to see the surprise." We headed to Delta City in Jill's car; it's about a twenty minute drive. We ended up at the High School, as I walked in; I knew what the surprise was. She had the keys to the school, and as we went inside, there were pictures of the faculty on the wall. There was a picture of Jill smiling face looking at me and underneath it said "Principal." Jill was promoted to Principal of the Delta High. I'm so proud of her; she has worked hard to get the position. We hugged; I told her how great she will be at the job and how proud I was of her. As we headed back to my folks home, she was telling me about all her plans she has for the school. When we drove up to the house, she started laughing from happiness, I think. They had put up a sign saying "Congratulation on your Promotion!"

It was great, for the rest of the day we relaxed at the folks place. We played around in the yard; we played yard darts, horse shoes, badminton and anything else we could come up with. The grandkids enjoy playing and petting the live stock. Dad and Mom had baby lambs, chickens, pigs and calves, which all the kids enjoyed. Daniel, Douglas and Tina all wanted to milk the cows. They did pretty well for their first time. Grandpa showed them how to pump their tails to get the milk going. He had them going for a little bit, but Grandpa couldn't help laughing. One thing about having city slicker around, they are easy to mess with, he always said.

The folks had a pond out back, so we went swimming and laid out in the sun enjoying the day. Dad told the kids to try and catch a couple of frogs for dinner. The kids all said "No thank you, to the eating of the frogs!" But they did have a blast trying to catch the frogs.

This evening the kids put on a talent show on for us, even our kids got involved in it. It was great! The little ones danced and sang, our kids sang "We ain't got a barrel of money." We did a sing along, and turned up the radio and started dancing around. I miss this place; I have a lot of great memory here. I'm glad the grandkids could spend some time with my parents. This trip was a great idea.

It's pretty late, Frank is already asleep, I haven't seen too much of him lately. His been running around with the guys and I've been hanging out with the women. He helped Dad fix a few things around the place. One thing about Frank he can fix anything. As much as I hate to say good-bye to my family, we'll be heading out tomorrow.

CHAPTER 13

Day 12

After a good night's sleep we hit the road. No one was hungry, so we decided to have breakfast on the road. We did have our coffee though. All the younger grandkids were still asleep in our R.V. Five hours later we spotted a campground just outside of a small town, called Austin. It's a living ghost town, but it has a nice looking RV campground.

I was driving so Frank called everyone on the walkie talkie to let they know we decided to stop at the campground and get settled in for the night. One we get settled in we will go investigate the town. Frank Jr. had picked up a flyer when he went in to check us all in. While we were fixing lunch Frank Jr. read the flyer. It said the town was having a carnival and later a cowboy shoot out at three o'clock. It sounded like a lot of fun. Everyone was excited about going.

All the kids and grandkids wanted to go to the carnival and every one would meet at the Shoot Out. Frank and I decided to go have a couple beers at the saloon. There was quite a crowd of tourists, there was standing room only. We thought we would go over to the bar and get a pitcher of beer while we waited for a table. It so happened we were between too rough looking characters. They didn't look like tourists; they looked like they just came in off the desert. The one on the left side of Frank had just gotten his pitcher of beer. He was wearing a cowboy hat and had a long beard. He was holding the pitcher of beer high in the air above the heads of the people crowding around us. Apparently the guy next to him, bumped up against him. The next thing I knew I had a pitcher of beer pouring over my head! Frank yelled at him "Hey buddy watch it!"

Frank yelled pretty loud because it was so noisy. The guy with the empty pitcher turned around. The guy on the other side of me was laughing. Whiskers said "You think that's funny?" "Yeah you Knit Whit!" said the guy with the big nose. Whiskers stepped out from behind Frank still holding on to the empty pitcher. Whiskers saw Frank grinning and took a left hand swing at him, Frank ducked. Big Nose got it right in the jaw and staggered a little, shook his head and rubbed his jaw. Then he charged Whiskers and knocked him down with a head butt.

By this time the crowd was getting excited. I was leaning over the bar trying to get the hair out of my face. Whiskers got up and went after Big Nose and hit him on the head with the glass pitcher. He was staggering around with blood running down the side of his head. Where the Sheriff came from I don't know. He was trying to stop the fight. I was afraid to move; Frank took a hold of me and was trying to get me out of the way. Everyone was yelling and trying to help the Sheriff.

The next thing I knew the four of us were hauled off to jail. It was some time later that the Sheriff came and unlocked the door of our cell and came in to talk to us. He wanted to hear our side of the story. By this time my hair had dried to a sticky mess. I must have looked a sight. We told him our side of the story. The Sheriff looked at us, then grinned and gave a little laugh. He said "Don't worry this isn't the first time these two have been in trouble. You two can go now, I guess you would like to get your hair washed Mrs. Smith."

As we came out of the jail house we heard gun shots! The Sheriff headed for his horse that was at the hitching rail in front. He jumped on his horse and headed down the street as he pulled out his pistols. He fired two shots in the air as he rode down the main street. The outlaw cowboys were out in the street, firing at the Bank and two deputies. The deputies were at the side of the Bank. The robbers saw the Sheriff and turned to fire at him. One by one the outlaws went down! The battle was won! The Sheriff dismounted and fired one more shot in the air. It was the signal, the outlaws got up, and the deputies came out into the street. They all took a bow. Everyone clapped. The actors headed to the saloon.

At first I was startled, and I had jumped behind Frank. Frank said "That was great!" I looked up at Frank and realized he had a black eye. I asked him what happened to your eye. He looked at me and replied "I guess I must have hit the side of my eye on the bar as I ducked, quite a shiner huh?" I think he was proud of it! He took my arm and said "Come on honey lets go find the kids." As I wrinkled up my nose I said "I'm really going to get teased about my hair!" "Well you know what they say about beer, it's good for your hair." Frank said with a chuckle.

About that time the kids found us, and had lots of questions for us. Frankie just said, "I can't leave you alone for a minute!" Frank replied, "That's right partner, you never know what your Ma and me might get into." The grandkids thought that was funny, and told Grandpa how cool his black eye looked. I asked, what about my new hairdo? Wanda spoke up, "I love it, where can I get it done? I told her lets go to the bar and I'll show you! No thanks, she replied.

"Well people, since we didn't get our beer at the saloon, let's go over to the beer garden that I saw earlier." Frank said. I replied "Ok by me, no one seems to notice my beer hair so I don't care. Let's go."

All the adults went for beer while the grandkids went over to the carnival for more rides. The older grandkids promised to look after them.

Well we are in Austin, so we went to an outdoor restaurant that had a live band and a pig on the fire. We had a great time, James ordered his steak well done, and when the food came out, they had an old boot for him instead of his steak. They told him we don't do well done, and handed him a medium rare steak. The owner said, "If you don't love it, you won't have to pay for it." Needless to say, we paid for it, it was really good! The steaks were tender, it just melted in your mouth, and everything else was great. The rest of the night we drank beer and danced. Daniel and Tina took the little ones home around 10:00. Twila and Maria walked them home and got everyone settled in and then came back.

As the evening went on, Frank pointed to two guys that were sitting at the bar. All I could say was, "I'll be damn!" It was the two guys from the bar fight earlier today. It looked like they were the best of friends. Then they spotted us, and they started to come over to us. Frank wasn't sure what was going to happen next. They both had big smiles on their faces, and put their hands out, offering to shake hands with us. Whiskers said, "Sorry about the black eye buddy!" Big Nose looked at me and said "Sorry about the hair ma' am." Then he said "I'm Jessie and this here is Tex. I looked at Big Nose; I mean Jessie and asked what happened to your nose? "Oh it's in my pocket ma' am, all part of the show." Jessie replied. I said "I Guess the bloody cut was a part of the show too huh Tex?" Tex replied with a sheepish grin "Shore enough ma' am. They laughed and started to take off. Then they turned around and said nice meeting you all. Oh yea, we ordered a round of drinks for ya' all. Big Nose joked or we could start another bar fight! Frank and I both said at the same time, "A drink sounds good, thanks! Twila said "We didn't hear about the bar fight!" I said that's not all and winked at Frank. I told Frank, Weird Right? But nice of them buy us all a drink. The rest of the evening was nice; we danced and enjoyed hanging out with our kids.

Another great vacation day, I can't wait to see what happens next. Eureka, CA is our next stop; we're going to have to get up pretty early to get there at a decent hour. Eureka is where Frank's parents live! The good news is they have a place already for us to park our trailers.

CHAPTER 14

Virginia City, NV
Day 13

Fallon, UT we ran into thousands of Monarch butterflies, they were migrating from Mexico. We were killing a lot of them; they would hit the front of our vehicles'. The little ones were getting upset, so we pulled off the side of the road and stopped. It was very cool to see all of the butterflies. We stood outside the cars, and the butterflies would just land on us. The grand girls really enjoyed it, the guys not so much. It was more of "Look what they did to my windshield, now I'm going to have to clean it!" We waited for the butterflies to pass by and then we headed to Reno. But before we left, we all had to wash our windshields.

We had talked about Virginia City, NV to our kids, but we never took them. They all voted to go there; it's a great little town. It is still alive and well. The last time Frank and I were there, there was no shortage of Saloon; they are all in full swing. I had to wonder if it had changed much in ten years.

We parked the rigs at a truck stop outside of Reno; there was a parking area outside of town, we could use. We all loaded up into two cars. It won't take long to get to the Virginia City, from the parking lot.

It was a nice day, it wasn't too hot and there was a little breeze, it was just enough to keep the heat off. I forgot how small the road was going up to Virginia City. I'm glad we didn't bring the rigs up here. We parked by the cemetery, we wanted to check out later. There are two cemeteries here, one is called Silver Terrace and the other is the Pioneer cemetery. I guess one filled up, so they had to open another one.

I can't help it; I need to put a little history about Virginia City. "Virginia City sprang up as a boomtown with the 1859 discovery of the Comstock Lode. The first major silver deposit discovery in the United States, and numerous mines were opened. At the city's peak of population in the mid-1860s, it had an estimated 25,000 residents. The mines' output declined after 1878, and the city declined." As usual, I found this information at the visitor center.

They really have worked hard to retain its authentic historic character with board sidewalks on both sides of the main street, and they have restored building all around the town. There are still lots of saloon in their town, the names were interesting. There was: Brass Rail Saloon, Long Branch Saloon, Red Dog Saloon and the one we had a drink in was the Bucket of Blood Saloon. We saved the beer bottle from that saloon; it had the name of the saloon on the beer bottle.

As we walked around they had live music in the different Saloons. We went into the Long Branch. We heard music coming out of there; we were expecting to see adults on the stage singing. But instead it was three little girls, from 7 to 10 years old. They were singing country songs from Reba and Dolly, it was amazing. Their voices sounded just like the stars of the song they were singing. I could of stay there and listen to them all night, but we needed to move on.

It's amazing how many things there are to do in this little town. We knew we would all get separated, so we all agreed to meet back at the graveyard by five. We still had to get to our next stop. Frank and I walked down the street, and looked in the windows. I had to wonder what kind of life it was back then. I think I would rather be stranded on the island with Frank, than live in a town like this back then.

The graveyards were pretty interesting, they had iron rod fencing around, some of the graves. A lot of the head stone you couldn't read what they said. The ones you could they had things like: Here lies Lester Moore four slugs from a 44, No Les No More, Stabbed by Gold Dollar, and the last one was Marshall White shot by Curly Bill.

We heard there were ghost here, but we didn't see anyone that looked like one. Frankie found one grave that not only had iron rod around the grave, it also had iron rod on top. It looked like a cage. Frankie remarked, "I guess they really wanted to make sure he didn't get out!" All of a sudden the wind picked up and tumbleweed hit Frankie on the side of his leg. I told him, you better watch out what you say here! He smiled and said, "Maybe so, let's go!"

After we walked around the grave yards, we loaded up and headed back to the rigs. Everyone had eaten in Virginia City, so we didn't have to stop and eat before we headed over the mountain. I wish we had more time. There is so much to see and do here, as I said earlier. Virginia City is neither dead nor abandoned by any means.

We made pretty good time until we hit the mountain range. It was a two lane road, and uphill. There is nothing like a big mountain range, to slow your rigs down. We stopped at the state park and because Seamore was starting to overheat and the kids were getting a little restless, there was a nice little creek to play in.

Frankie told them there might be gold in it. That's all it took. It was beautiful, the trees were pines and redwoods, and they were huge. Well for even Texans they were huge! It was so peaceful, besides the kids playing; all we heard was a woodpecker somewhere out there. We could hear the sounds of the creek and the wind moving the branches of the trees. We stayed and enjoyed it for about 30 minutes and then we were back on the road. We still had a long ways to go before we arrived in Eureka, CA.

Eureka is right on the coast, Frank's parent have lived there for thirty years. They moved there after Dennis, Frank's Dad, retired from the Army. Eureka received its name from a Greek word meaning "I have found it!" "It was founded in 1850 by the Union and Mendocino Exploring companies. The Wiyot people lived in Jaroujiji (Wiyot "where you sit and rest") the area now known as Eureka, for thousands of years prior to European arrival. The entire city is a state historic landmark, which has hundreds of significant Victorian homes."

As we headed to Eureka there were a lot of ups and downs in the Sierra Nevada mountain range. It is the mountain range between Nevada and California and runs from one end of CA and down into Mexico. Going down hills we made pretty good time, but going uphill Seamore would have a hard time. We had to turn off the air conditioner, the engine had more power and wouldn't over heat. Once we started going down the hill I would turn the air back on and when we started going up a hill I would turn it off. It was about 90 degrees outside, it felt like it was a lot hotter in Seamore. I don't mind heat, but not in a vehicle.

Frank and I have been through these mountain ranges a few times through the years. But this is the first time we have taken a RV over the mountain. It so different than a car, you can see over the bushes. You can see so much farther! In a car you can only see things by the road. But in the RV we can see over the bushes. When you're in a car you are missing the views and the beauty of the mountains.

In some cases I could see for miles. I wanted to stop and show the kids, but there was no place to pull over. I'm really glad we are driving the RV, instead of one of the cars that are pulling the trailers. One of the bigger problems is there really wasn't any place for all of us to stop. The only break we got was at the gas station. We had dinner at a truck stop, which was right off the freeway. One thing, what they say about truck stops food is right, it was great! We went to the gift shop and everyone picked up a souvenir. The little ones wanted toys, instead of a souvenir, it wasn't any fun.

As we headed to Eureka, CA, we did hit some flat land for about two hours, and then we hit the Coast Mountains. It was mostly uphill in the beginning but once we got to the top it was all downhill. By then it was around 6:00 p.m. and had cooled off. The mountain ranges were totally different than anything in Texas. The grandkids haven't been this far north, so they watched out the window. Every time they saw a deer, elk or even squirrels they would let us know. They couldn't believe how big the trees were, we don't have anything like this in Texas.

We had all six of the Grandkids in Seamore and I was driving. So Grandpa was in charge of keeping the kids entertained. Grandpa kept telling them stories; one thing I heard was "You haven't seen anything yet! Wait until you see the real Redwood trees, they were here when the dinosaurs roamed the earth. The younger ones would ask him, really? That's all it took, Grandpa would start telling stories about this or that.

We arrived at Frank's parent house around 9:00 p.m. There was just his folks' Dennis and Lola at their home. There was lots of hugging. Both our families love to hug each other. Lola (Mom) told us everyone would be coming tomorrow; they figured we would be pretty tired. We both thanked them, it has been a long day, and I was looking forward to going to bed. It was around 11:00 when I said my good nights. Frank on the other hand, wanted to stay up and catch up with his parent's. Well he did get a nap in today. I told Frank, I wanted to catch up on my journal and then hit the sack! Our kids were finishing setting up their trailers and getting the kids settled in for the night. Once our grandkids were all snuggled in their beds, our kids joined us.

All of the adults were outside enjoying the beautiful sunset. We were all relaxed enjoying the peace and quiet of the evening.

I looked around and thought how fortunate Frank and I are. Here we were safe at home with our family.

The girls: Lola (Frank's Mom) Wanda, Twila, and Maria decide to go get some sleep. Their kids had really kept them busy. The guys Dennis (Dad), Frank, Frankie, Dennis and James were sitting around talking quietly and every once in awhile I would hear them chuckling about something one of them had said.

I looked at Frank, he was laughing and he looked so happy and content. I was sitting a little bit away from them. I was in a quite mood, feeling sad and guilty at the same time. I kept comparing how different our life was now. I was having a hard time putting the Roslanders out of my mind. I thought I have to stop thinking this way and concentrate on our life now.

I can understand that being stranded on the island for so long, it would be hard to adapt to this world again. I have such a wonderful family. I feel like I haven't been a good mother, taking off like we did. I felt my eyes were starting to tear up. I wonder if I'll ever leave the guilt behind and be a better mother and grandmother.

CHAPTER 15

Day 14
Eureka, CA

Waking up and hearing the ocean first thing in the morning made me feel so much better. I guess some days I just miss the island and that makes me feel guilty. Today Frank's brother Styles came to join us for breakfast; he lives on a research ship not too far from here. He told us this morning that he has gotten approval for us to go on board tomorrow. He figures we would like to just hang out around Eureka, and visit with the folks and Frank's cousins. In Dennis's (Dad) family, there were two brothers and three sisters living in this area. That was the reasons Dennis and Lola moved here, when he retired from the Army. It was time to go home. As he would put it!

As long as we were so close to the Pacific Ocean, we all decided to go to the beach. It looked like it was going to be a nice day. Maybe we could do a little beach combing. It would be like old times for Frank and me.

After awhile we all headed to the beach. It was a beautiful day, it was sunny, and there was a cool breeze blowing. It was a weekday so there weren't a lot of people around. We packed a picnic lunch, and an ice chest with drinks. The nice thing was we could drive on the beach. I guess I'm getting lazy in my old age. We had to take three cars, so we parked them in a semi-circle on the beach. If the wind does pick up we'll have protection. Frank's folks were in there 80's, so we had a couple of chairs for them to sit on. Frank suggested we take some jackets with us, just in case it turned cold. It was still pretty early in the day so there still weren't many people on the beach.

Everyone was in a hurry to get down to the beach. It was wonderful just strolling along with Frank. We just kept smiling at each other, holding hands. As we were going along we spotted a small dog. It was just wandering along like it was looking for someone or something. We looked up and down the beach; we didn't see any one looking for it. It came up to us and Frank knelt down and the little guy jump up on Frank and crawled inside his nylon jacket. The dog looked like a miniature Grey Hound. It was so scared; you could tell it was lost.

We took him over to the car and fed him a hot dog. He was really hungry. I started calling him Little Bit. Frank just kept him in his jacket with the zipper up, but enough room to stick his head out. I was already getting attached, but I knew better. But I couldn't help it, Little Bit was so adorable. I told Frank that we should go to the police station to see what to do.

We talked to the kids and they agreed we should notify the police. They told us to take the van and they would wait for us at the beach. Of course, the grandkids wanted to keep Little Bit. We told them no way, someone loves him and no doubt they are looking for him.

It seems like Frank and I just keep rescuing animals on the beach. It would not leave Franks jacket, so I didn't get to hold it. Darn. We arrived at the Police station and the officer checked to see if there were any reports of missing dogs. We were in luck there was one that fit the description. He said it was rare that they ever got that kind of dog. The police officer called the owners and let them know that we had found their dog. When he talked to the owners, he told them where we would be parked on the beach. They said it would take about three hours to get here; we gave the Officer the address of Frank's parents, just in case it took them longer than three hours. According to the Officer, I guess they had been heading home, when they stopped at the beach. Something scared Little Bit, so he took off running, and just disappeared. They looked everywhere for him, all they could do is ask the police department to keep an eye out for him.

We went back to the beach and told everyone what happened. Little Bit just rode around in Frank's jacket most of the time. It was getting warm but Frank just kept his jacket on, he didn't what to upset Little Bit. After awhile Little Bit warmed up to Treva on the blanket. They had fallen asleep together, it was so cute. We all had a great time on the beach; we played football, surfing and did a little bit of fishing. We could see the sea lions playing in the water. There was about ten of them sunning themselves up the beach a little ways. They didn't care one way or another about us being there.

The three hours passed fairly fast, but Little Bits owners still hadn't showed up. It was time to head back to Frank's parent's house; we waited for them to arrive. We were playing cards when we heard a knock on the door. When we answered there stood an older couple holding a little dog. It was the same kind of dog as Little Bit. They introduced themselves as Mr. and Mrs. Tyler, we invited them in. The instant they were in, Little Bit just went crazy with happiness. They put the little female down on the couch with Little Bit. Frank had taken his jacket off and put it on the couch with Little Bit inside when we got back from the beach. He didn't move from there until the Tyler's showed up.

Frank told them how Little Bit wouldn't leave his jacket. Mr. Tyler grinned and said "That figures they both share our nylon sleeping bag at night. I guess that's why he wouldn't leave me, Frank replied. Mrs. Tyler said, "They are very close; I don't know how come he ran off." I asked what their names were. Mrs. Tyler replied "Seems like they are always getting into mischief so we named them Bonnie and Clyde." We all laughed. Mrs. Tyler also said "When Clyde got away from us; we spent two whole days looking for him. Bonnie was so upset she stopped eating. But now everything will be all right, thanks to you people! We would like to give you a reward. I said no, no, we enjoyed the little fellow.

We visited for a little while, and then they had to get going. We walked them out to the car to say goodbye. As we watched them drive off Bonnie and Clyde had their front paws on the dashboard looking out the windshield. They looked so happy; if they could have waved, I think they would have. After a little while Frank's family started showing up. He only had the one brother Styles, but his family made up for it with all his cousins. It was great fun, everyone was told to bring pictures of them when they were young and a picture of them now. They put it on a board Mom had put up. Everyone was laughing and pointing at each other. Mom, put one up of Frank and I on our wedding day. Man have we changed! I think she didn't want me to feel left out. All of the grandkids put their pictures up too. It was funny to see some of the grandkids pictures; they looked just like their uncle or aunt. They could have been their brother or sister.

Frank's folks had their backyard set up for parties. They had a pool table, horse shoes, and three other games that you used balls for and even with balls on a string. Their BBQ pit was big enough to cook a pig in, if they wanted to. From my understanding they have. Everyone was having a great time, when Cousin Chad suggested they go night fishing. So a bunch of them loaded up and headed to the beach. The rest of us hung out at the house and played cards, and other board games.

After about an hour the guys came back with a dozen fish. Dad started up the BBQ, while the guys cleaned the fish. Dad had made a holder to cook the fish in. All you have to do is flip them; it kind of looked like a net, but flat like a basket, made out of wirer. It was very cool!

After the fish was done cooking we sat around the table outside and ate. We had the fish and Mom had made homemade fries and garlic bread. There is nothing like fresh fish and chips! I ate way to much garlic bread. I think it was the only time everyone was quiet at one time.

People started leaving around 11:00 pm; we said our good-byes and invited everyone to come see us in Houston. They said they would, but to be honest, I doubt if they ever will.

We're looking forward to going on the research ship with Styles tomorrow. It was nice seeing Frank and his brother hanging out together, they don't get to do it very often. When we came up missing, Styles joined the search team to find us; he had told us earlier he had looked for months for us. Every island he saw, he would stop and search every inch of it for a clue.

CHAPTER 16

Day 15
Research Ship

S tyles had told us to meet him down at the docks in
Eureka. We would have a boat pick us up and bring
us out to the research vessel. Frank's folks said they
would watch the younger grandkids for us. Anyone under the
age of sixteen couldn't go. That let only the adults: Frank, me,
our kids and their partners, even that was a lot. Good thing
Styles sent a big boat.

The research boat was about an hour out to sea, so we
rode out on a smaller boat to reach the ship. I kept looking for
the Silver Merbeings; they had told us that they lived in these
waters. It's just a habit, for us to look for merbeings when we are
on the water. Frank poked me with his elbow; he knew what I
was doing. Then he said "See anything?" No, I replied!

When we arrived at the ship, Styles and his wife Lucy and their two boys Tony and Adam were there to welcome us aboard. The whole family went into the research business. We found out later that they own the vessel; it is not called a ship.

The vessel was incredible; it had everything a research vessel would need. It is 209' long and has a complete wet dry laboratories, it had scientific lab, charts, drafting room, a machine shop and all kinds of other things. Most of it went over my head, but it all sounds very important.

After we toured the vessel, Style ordered them to start the engines and head someplace, he gave coordinates to them. Next thing I knew we were headed south. Lucy came up to me and told me, "Wait until you see us in action, it's much cooler." I asked her, what are we going to do? She said, "Just wait and see! We have to get things ready so we're going to take you to the Captain quarters. We'll come get you when we're ready"

The Captain quarters were bigger than I imagined, and was nicer than Seamore in space. Lucy told us to make ourselves comfortable, it shouldn't take too long. Tony and Adam will be up shortly to give you instruction on what you will be doing. We all just smiled and looked at each other wondering what was going on. I could tell by the expression on Frank's face, he knew something. After Lucy left I turned to Frank and asked him what's up? He just smiled and said you'll see, I promised I wouldn't say anything.

It wasn't long until Adam and Tony showed up. They had brochures that had information about the research vessel and some training material. In the brochures it explained what this vessel was used for. According to the information we got from the guys, "This ship collects gravity and magnetic data from the sea floor. They also create seismic images of rock layers below the ocean floor; dredged rock samples; and took ocean floor sentiment cores, mapped the ocean floor with sonar. Collect water samples to explore ocean currents, temperature, salinity, marine life, and other data for a wide range of oceanographic research"

Then they explained to us that we would be taking samples for their next project. We would be partnered up with an experienced person from the vessel and we would be in groups of four. They showed us the different containers that they would be using and instructed us if we saw anything unusual to let the cameraman know, he would take a picture of it. Once we discovered what we were going to do, we all got really excited. We waited for Lucy to come back and get us.

After awhile the engine stopped and Lucy came over and asked us to come with her. They had scuba gear for all us, she told us to suit up, were going to go for a swim. She introduced us to our team leader, and broke us into groups. Our whole family has been scuba diving for most of our lives. This was something we have done before but to do it professionally and collect specimens is definitely a change for us.

There were large amounts of plants and sea life here. Julio the team leader gave us each tasks to do. I was in charge of collecting plants and small creature I might find. As we broke off into our teams, Frankie, Wanda, our leader Julio and I were on the same team. Each of us had a grid that we were responsible for. For the rest of the afternoon we collected and returned to the vessel with our container filled. Then we would go back down and collect more samples. It was a great day, I even made a friend it was a seal, and it looked pretty young. He would follow me around and help me pick up ideas, it was the funniest thing. He even gave me a fish once; I took it and then gave it back to him.

That evening we ate a light meal on the vessel and talked about the day. Styles said, "We did great, and if we ever wanted a job, come see him." We all laughed and said no thanks. Believe it or not it's a lot of hard work. It was good seeing how Frank's brother and his family lived. They seemed to be very happy and enjoyed what they do for a living.

Styles and Lucy asked if we could talk in private, we said sure. After we went into one of the conference room, and sat down. Styles went right to the point. I've heard stories from my grand niece Cheryl, about the Roslanders, they are merbeings, Correct! Sharlene and Cheryl write to each other every week. Sharlene tells her all the stories you tell her and the other grandkids. Frank and I weren't sure what to do.

I guess our faces showed what we were thinking. Lucy spoke up, "We're not upset, just the opposite! To make a long story short, we have seen them too!" We were doing some research in the Atlantic, when we first saw them. In the beginning when we were setting up the equipment, we would see them watching us. But once we started doing the testing, they disappeared. We were afraid that we may have been the cause of it, but we had to finish the testing."

Then Styles, who is just like his brother Frank, went straight to the point. "Did you really know merbeings or were they just stories?" We didn't know what to say, but we did know it was important for them to know that the test they did hurt the merbeings. We asked if we could have a minute and they agreed.

As they were walking out Lucy said, "Whatever you tell us, it won't go any further, you have our word on it!"

It didn't take long for us to agree that we need to tell them about the merbeings. They needed to stop whatever testing they were doing that hurt the merbeings. We asked them to come back in, and we told them the story the Sanderlander's told us. There are many different clans, but the clans you are talking about are called the Sanderland. It is important for you to understand things about them. The Chief did have a message for the humans, so we feel it is the right thing to do, is to tell you their whole story. But as Lucy said earlier, you can't repeat this to anyone.

The Sanderland story

Their Chief's name is Ndsa and his partners name is Losa. They have been together for many years, and they have five children which are all grown up. Three of their children had moved to other clans, but two of them came with them to the Batjak. Batjak is a festival they have each year to celebrate life.

The Sandlander Merbeings do not look the same as the other clans we have met. The colors are different from the other clans we have seen. The under part of their bellies are a sand color, and a creamy gray on the sides. Their tail is not as wide as the other merbeings either. Their tails are brown with red on them, not spots, but inside the tail. Their head crown on the males is higher in the front and goes down their back, whereas the females head crown are about an inch all the way down the middle of their head, going down to their neck.

I asked them to tell me about their homeland. Chief Ndsa said that their homeland and the city under the water are in the same area. They travel back and forth on a day-to-day basis.

The water is very deep in their city under the water. The city on land, Sandland, sits on top of an extinct volcano. The mass of the mountain is below water, but the top of the volcano is about two miles above the surface of the water. Access to the Sandland City is by way of a subterranean tunnel, and you can surface near the center of the city, near the Circle of Life. They live on the side of the mountain, a lot like the cities that humans have on the water's edge. Their homes are made of earth, and the gardens are in between the homes. The island and the city are protected by the Circle of Life. The Circle of Life is what protects them from humans and other creatures.

Their homeland also has access via the rivers that are made from the waterfalls that come down the mountain range; the water flows into the pool inside the city and then goes down the mountain to an underwater waterfall.

There are caves throughout the volcano, and they can travel around inside of the mountain where many of them live. The caverns are huge; some rooms are three floors high. There is a pool inside of the cavern, which is warmed by the volcano. (Frank said, it sounded like a Turkish bathhouse.) There are large mineral stones all around, there are caves going off to other rooms, where the stones are grown for the Circle of Life.

As you come out below their caverns, you can see their underwater city in the distance; you can see a faint glow. They had to build their underwater city in deeper water just in case their above ground city was discovered.

Ndsa explained to us how full of life the water is. He said there are many different types of fish and plants, some of which he is sure Frank and I have never seen before. Their sea plants are as big as fir trees! They wave in the water back and forth, just like the wind does to the trees on land. There are sharks of all kinds, but everyone just lives together peacefully.   It was wonderful that by using the communication connection with the merbeings, we could see everything they saw and told us about. It was as if we were watching a movie, and the narrator was talking to us.

Losa told us there is a place where the sharks come to rest and have their babies near the city. We leave them alone and the sharks leave us alone. The large plants are all hallow inside, the pipes are used to bring warm water into the city. The underwater city is called Sandpiper and the city on the land is called Sandland.

Sandland was used by the merbeings and the gray ones (which I think is same thing as the green ones). Losa called them star beings, the way she described them it sounded a lot like the green ones, but only gray. It also sounded like they still visited them off and on. Losa and Ndsa were not willing to talk about them in detail. All they would say is they lived even deeper in the water than any merbeings do and their machines can go on land, water and into the darkness, what humans call the sky.

Ndsa continued to tell us, the island used to be bigger than it is now. The star beings used to live in the caverns you saw earlier, they were above the water, but as the water came they moved to higher land, so we moved our clan into the caverns. All of the water channels on their island were made by the star being too, so they would have easy access to the land and the water.

For many years the humans didn't come into our waters, and there was no other land around. We assumed there was no point in fearing the humans, they wouldn't come here!

Then we noticed some big ships started coming into the area. On their first visit, they just dove and searched below the water, but we didn't know what for. Fortunately, the humans could not see their city because it was protected by the Circle of Life. The merbeings stayed out of sight, until the humans left. On their second visit, they started sending out sound waves, almost like the call of whales. Then they started using longer and higher pitched sound waves. We had to move everyone to the island out of the water, because of the sound.

After the humans were gone, we all had head pains and some of the merbeings ears were bleeding. After their third visit I commanded everyone to move on to the island, before they started their testing again. Each time they visited they would stay longer and longer, cause more and more problems.

The humans showed up again but this time they brought four ships. I gathered up the clan and we immediately moved out of the area and into Utopia City.

They had to move to Utopia to get away from it. It had been a major hardship for the old and little ones of the clan. Normally, we didn't have to travel long distances, but in this case we had no choice. We needed to get away from the sound waves, before there was any more damage to the clan.

It had been three months since they moved and the ships were still there. He would have their scouts go and check to see if the sound waves are still there, but they can't get close enough to see the ships, because the sound waves are so strong. The scouts came back with headaches and other hearing problems. Whatever, the humans are doing it is dangerous for the merbeings and other sea creatures.

As the human continue to push us farther out into the ocean and take over our islands, we have been working on our new city under the water. The last time the Star beings visited the Sandlanders, they helped them hide their city deeper on the bottom of the water. They showed us how to make waterfalls under the water, to draw light from above deeper down to the city, so we wouldn't miss the land features.

Ndsa started to explain how they did it, "The tall plants are hollow in the middle. So we cut them in half and placed them length wise, next to each other, and lay them on the cliff. Then we adjust the air pressure just right and it gives the look of a waterfall."

We may be water beings, but we do enjoy the beauty of the land. As we move farther out into the deep water, we see less and less of the land features. The islands they use for sunbathing are much smaller now because of the rising water, so there's not much left to see of them.

They have water tunnels that they use to go in-land, where there are lakes. They sound a lot like roads on land, where some of the roads are open and then others have tunnels you have to drive through. We have the same thing where we can swim for a very long ways in the open. Yet there will be tunnels that we have to swim through to get to the lakes.

As our people move deeper into the water, we still need to absorb the sun for our bodies. We can float on the surface of the water, but that is dangerous because of predators or even the humans may see us. We have come up with devices under the sea to help with this problem but there is nothing like sitting on a rock and enjoying the sun. The device, which looks like algae to humans, floats on the surface of the water and absorbs the sun and then pass the energy to the next plate, which looks like sea plants, and then the energy it receives from the sun to an absorbing box. Then we can lie on flat stone and the box will cover us in sun energy.

At one time, all merbeings lived in the same area. But as the clans grew, and the planet started to change and the earth moved and destroyed part of the city, it was decided they needed to separate to protect their race.

As the years passed the connection was lost between some of the clans. The merbeings had to adapt to the new areas they lived in. Sandlander Clan changed their color to match the area around them. After many years, the clan had grown so large, that they had to find a bigger city to live in. They found not far from their old home and that is where they live now. At least until the ships came and chase them out to Utopia. We hope in time we can go back there, but until the ships leave we can't.

The one thing that Ndsa the Chief of Sanderland wanted us to tell the humans was, "It was important for the humans to understand that there are intelligent creatures in the ocean, and that they needed to stop testing bombs and other sound weapons in the water. Ndsa said the new sound machines the humans are testing was causing the merbeings major problems! They had to move to Utopia city, which is deep in the ocean, just so they could get away from the sound. We are hoping that they will be done with their testing by the time we go home."

The testing stopped not too long after we had talked to Ndsa and Losa, we were told through the grape vine. But the damage had been done, a few of the Scout's and the older being had lost their hearing. They're not sure what other damaged it had caused.

Many sea creatures had left the area, and haven't returned yet. This could be a problem, because it was their food supply.

Styles and Lucy pretty much had the same expression that we had, the first time we saw Tride (our first merman). Then they looked at each other and at the same time said, "I knew it!" After they settled down, they thanked us for sharing the information with them. We knew the testing must have been hurting the sea life. We had no idea it was hunting the Merbeings. Styles told us, "Just so you know we were not part of the last four ships. We refuse to do anymore testing in that area, and tried to stop the rest of the testing. They were going to put a ship there for a year, but at least we stopped that."

Frank and I was so surprise that they had seen merbeings and wanted to help them too. Small world! For the next hour we talked about the different clans, and the different areas they lived. It was wonderful to talk to someone about how wonderful the Merbeings were. We told them we would have never survived without them.

Frank asked them, "Had they seen any other odd thing while they were out on the ocean. Almost together they said "Yes! There were some huge mass of blue algae, and it was so thick we couldn't go through it. We tried to go around it, but it had to be at least 30 miles long and 10 miles across. We did testing and there really wasn't anything abnormal about it. There was a big storm coming in so we had to move out of its way. When we returned the next day, the blue algae's was gone. We have no idea where it went." Then they had the same look and said "Why?" Frank told them "No reason." I told them we had heard from the Roslanders that there was a blue algae mass, which was growing larger than anything they had seen before. We were just wondering if you had seen it too.

Style and Lucy said, "Oh, as far as the testing goes, we do have some pull now. They would try and get that type of testing stopped. They won't tell anyone what we had talked about, but there is other ways to get the testing stopped."

Lucy had one more question, "Are there Merbeings on the California coast line. All we could do is say, yes they are called Catilander. We haven't seen any since we been here. Style replied, "We have, from a distance! It was funny; we all had smiles on our faces, like a little kid that had a secret we had to keep.

It was getting late and we needed to get back to the grandkids. Styles and his family rode back to Eureka with us, and the Folk's and grandkids were waiting at the docks for us. To our surprise, Tony and Adam had caught lobsters and crabs for dinner. The folk's and grandkids had caught some fish. Seafood all around, this time Mom made potatoes salad and coleslaw to go along with it. I love this vacation; I hardly ever cook or clean. The grandkids clean up Seamore, I just have to keep our bedrooms clean, and Franks helps with that.

As usual dinner was great and everyone talked about the adventures we had on the ship. All the kids were asking their parents questions about what they did and what they found. Frank and I just sat there and enjoyed our wonderful family; we could hear the ocean in the back ground.

Tomorrow we're heading to the Redwood National Park. The folk's, Styles and his family and all of our clan will be going. Another day gone and another great day it was!

CHAPTER 17

Day 16
Redwood National Forest

As we were sitting around at breakfast, Styles asked Frank about the dream room on Rosland Island. He had heard that we had found this ancient building inside the mountain there. "That's where you guys found it, right? So my question is, "What did you see in your dream room?

Frank told him, "It was so real, in a matter of thirty minute, I had seen us as kids and enjoying the Redwood forest, like we used to. Remember how we would go to the one tree and try to reach each other's hands around the tree. But we never did. We knew we couldn't but it was funny trying. But I also saw a tree house with a rope going up to it. I climbed it and could see the fields in the distance. We always wanted a tree house, and what better place than in a tall Redwood tree!

Lucy said "Well we know one thing we need to do now while we're in the Redwood forest. You guys need to try to reach each other around the tree again. Dad and Mom agreed, but we need to do it with each of the family and take lots of pictures. Everyone agreed it sounded like fun.

Before we left to go to the Redwoods, we broke down Seamore and the trailers. When we get back from the Redwoods, we wanted to get going on our trip. Of course the Redwoods are in the opposite direction than where we would be going next. We headed to Crescent city; it took us a little over an hour and half to get there.

I've only been there once before. Frank and I had been married for two years and we were on our way to his new duty station at Ft. Bliss, TX. We had stopped in the Redwood forest on our way to see his parents.

We had two vans, Styles had a big van that they used to transport personnel to job sites, and we used Frankie van. We entered the park, and the grandkids were surprised to see how huge the Redwoods were. Grandpa Frank told them, "You haven't seen anything yet!" The deeper in the park you drive the bigger the trees get.

We found the area where Frank's family had gone before, when he was a little boy. They weren't sure which tree it was, so they just picked one. Everyone piled out and was looking up into the trees. As little Treva was looking up into the trees, she started to fall backward, but James caught her. Then they got the great idea of lying down and looking up into the trees. So there we were, with six kids laying on the ground and two adults. Dennis, Twila's husband and Frank joined them on the ground. Then we tried the reaching around the tree. Frank, Dad, Styles and Mom were first. The tree they picked was too big, so Frank called our kids and Styles boys to join them. Sure enough that was enough people to go around the tree. With our arms stretch out and holding each other hand, we did it.

After having fun taking turns trying to circle the tree, we went to the tourist area. There is a tree with a large hole that goes right through the middle of the huge tree; you can drive right through it too. Style's van was too big so he couldn't drive through the tree. We loaded all the grandkids into Frankie van, so at least they could do it. All of the adults stood on the other side and took pictures. We had found a nice place to have a picnic, the kids ran around and played hide-seek.

As I was taking pictures I couldn't believe how much they all looked like each other. Frank looked like his Dad, tall, dark black hair and dark brown eyes, where Style his brother, looked like his Mom, light brown hair, with blue eyes, he wasn't as tall as Frank but he was almost 6 foot.

We headed back to Eureka around 2, picked up our rigs (RV and trailers) then headed to Salina, CA. We stopped outside of Salina; there was this really nice RV Campground that was right on the beach. Frank's family had stayed there a few times when they were young. We wanted to enjoy one more day on the Pacific coast.

Frank and I talked about taking a boat out by ourselves and calling for the Silver Merbeings (Catilander). They had told us that their clan lived in this area. The evening was nice and warm. We couldn't stand it, so we rented a boat and headed out into the ocean. Once we were out far enough Frank dived into the water and called to the Merbeings, hoping they would come. We waited in the boat and after awhile, we saw dolphins and then a group of fish. The dolphins acted like they were checking us out. We tried communication with them the way we did on the Rosland Island. At first they acted surprised and swam under the boat and then came back up and started talking to us. We only know Merbeings sounds, and some of the sounds for other sea creatures. After a little while, they disappeared.

Frank wanted to try one more time; he got back into the water. This time he told them our names and we had been on Rosland Island and lived with the Roslanders. He climbed back into the boat and waited, at first we saw a group of tuna swimming by us. Then the dolphins came back, this time giving us a little show, they did a couple of flips and rode on their tails backwards. It was their way of saying hi to us.

Then we saw them, two Merbeings, in the beginning they didn't get to close to us. But I telecommunicated with them that we would like to talk to them. I told them, we had talked to Hica and Prca when we lived on Rosland Island, with the Roslanders. Hica and Prca had told us about their clan that lives in this area. All of a sudden they pop up right next to the boat. I forgot how fast they could move.

It was a male and a female; they told us their names were Chca and Paul. I was surprised the male was named Paul. He smiled and said, "That is what the humans call me. We are friends with a few of them on the island. My real name is Syca, but you can call me Paul if you like. Chca said, "Hica is my brother, we haven't seen him in awhile. What did Hica tell you about us?" I asked is he ok? Chca said, "Yes, he is helping another clan out, their scout had been killed by a shark.

All I said was I'm so sorry, I didn't feel it was right to start questioning her about what clan, where, etc. Frank spoke up and said, "Your brother is a very brave being." Chca thanked him. Then Paul, spoke up "What did Hica and Prca tell you about us? I started telling them what they had told us:

Hica and Prca story!

Hica told us, "His clan is originally from the islands in the Pacific Ocean, and the majority of their clan is still there. They know the human name for the ocean where they live because they see and listen to humans quite a bit. Hica said, "The humans are always in the water or on the beaches there, and they are not very quiet about anything."

He explained to us that "The Traveler's" from the Catilander Clan is only made out of single merbeings; we are what humans would call Nomads. They travel around the world and visit other clans, and as they travel to the different clans, sometimes they do have other clan members join them. They use the ocean currents to make it easier and faster for them to travel so extensively. They also use the ships as another way of traveling. The human ships are so large, that they can attach to the side of one and no one knows they are there. They also swim with dolphins and whales. There are so many ways that they travel through the waters and yet the humans never see them.

They spend most of their lives around humans, and most of the time they don't even know they are around. The humans that do see them, they befriend them and they keep it to themselves, because they don't want people to bother us or think they are crazy.

What humans call, California and Mexico that is where our city located. It is in the deep waters. It is only their home base of sorts, as they are hardly ever there. It is a place mostly for the older merbeings in our clan that have finished their travels and have settled down with a partner. Our parents live there and other family members.

Because there are so many humans in the area, they have to stay underwater, and it is hard for them to do any sunbathing, (as we already know sunbathing is very important for merbeings). To make up for the loss, they have built rooms that they can use to absorb sun. This is done by using mirrors directing the sun into the areas that they want the heat and the sun to shine. Most of the mirrors have been made by humans and they just pick them off of boats and ships on the ocean floor.

The first time they discovered that they could use the mirrors it was a long time ago, and it had burnt one of the mermaids. The mermaid thought she could see another mermaid far away in the distance. She didn't realize it was her own reflection. As she got closer to the minor the sun came out from behind a cloud and when it hit the mirror, it sent a light beam directly at her! Needless to say she was quite surprised, and did not know how great a thing she had discovered.

The mermaids took the mirror back to the city and showed it to the elders. She told them what had happened and what the mirror could do. They called in the engineers and they went right to work on figuring out how they could incorporate it into their city. I thought to myself, they really are a lot like us!

The order went out to find as many of the mirrors as they could. In the past, they had never really paid attention to where they had seen the mirrors. Through the years, they developed their use of the mirrors, and stones, to help them with receiving the heat and sunlight that they need.

Prca told us, "We are called the Traveler's, our clan is younger merbeings; we travel and map out the waters around the world. There are many water tubes (caves) throughout the world, most of which are made from natural processes, but there are also water tubes that have been made by others, so that they can travel without being seen by anyone. These water tubes cut their travel time down by quite a bit. Once they enter the water tube, the water moves quickly so it feels like they are being shot through the tube. The next thing they know they come out on the other side.

They also visit different clans to see how things are going, and to make sure that they are still in their original location. As they get older each Catilander merbeings serves as scouts. They learn as much as they can about each of the clans through their travels, so when the time comes we are promoted to Scouts. Then we will be ready to assist in other merbeings making important decisions in their travels. It is important for them to know how many clans are out there, and where they are located so their maps are accurate.

In addition, if they have to take a group to another clan, they know where they are and what danger to look out for, and they can make sure to have enough scouts trained for the future.

Prca also told us, Scouts are highly regarded, and are very strong and can sense danger. When you turn five; you are trained to listen to your senses, and to be aware of everything around you. At the age of seven if you don't want to follow the path of a Scout, you didn't have too, but most did."

Chca replied, "I guess you did talk to Hica and Prca. You have a good understanding of our clan. What can we do for you?" Frank and I just smiled and said we just miss seeing and being with the Roslanders. Frank told them, "I think we just wanted to make sure we didn't imagine it all." Paul laughed and said "We get that a lot, but we are real and living right next to the humans. Chca said "We really can't tell you anything about the Roslanders or any other clans. It is not our place." We told her we understood, and started talking about other things. They told us about the humans they know, and other things about the people they communicate with. They didn't give us any names, but it was good to visit with them.

After awhile we said our good-byes and thanked them for coming. We asked them to pass a hello and tell the Roslanders that we are doing fine. Paul said he would.

When we got back the kids we're sitting around the campfire cooking hot dogs and marshmallows. They asked what we were doing out there; we just told them we missed being out in the water. Frank changed the subject, "Where should we stop next. Sharlene grabbed my hand and pulled me aside, and asked me, "Were there merbeings out there?" I smiled and said, what do you think? Sharlene was always the curious one. She said, "Yes, I'll keep your secret Grandma!" I thanked her, and gave her a kiss and a hug, before we walked back to the group.

To our shock Dennis, Twila husband, told us he had a surprise for us if we stopped at Bakersfield, CA. Dennis never said much, it normally was Twila.

"What kind of surprise? Frank asked. Dennis replied, It wouldn't be a surprise now would it Frank!" Ok Dennis that will be our next stop.

We headed out around 6:00 am, Dennis wanted to get to the surprise early enough to catch it. He had all of us wondering what was going on. Twila just smiled and said, "You'll see soon enough!"

When we arrived Dennis said, "Stop here, we have to walk a ways." Everyone was getting excited, now we have to wait here. We were in the middle of what seemed like nowhere. All there was were brushes, rocks and sand, it looked like a prairie. The grandkids were gathered all around us, not knowing what the surprise might be. After ten or fifteen minutes they started to wander.

About that time Douglas yelled, "Hey I found a snake!" Dennis told him don't tough it, leave it be. Then there were several more and then more and more. I said, "What's going on Dennis?" They are migrating Aggie! They are migrating from their hibernation sites to forging grounds but return to the same den site in the fall.

The questions started coming from all of us to Dennis. Oh my goodness, there looks like there are thousands of them.

What are they called? "Red-sided garter snakes"

Where do they come from? "These snakes overwinter in deep crevices formed in rocks and in sink holes in grassy pastures. Because suitable sites are rare, hundreds and sometimes thousands of snakes may be found in hibernacula. The females can give birth to 10 to 20 live young, there record is 100 young." What do they eat? Some of the things are frogs, bugs and leeches.

Many are killed on the roads and highways. The animal control tries to protect them the best they can by closing the highway till they cross.

Wow! You really know a lot about them Dennis, I told him. I've been around here for a very long time. I was raised over that hill there, as he pointed at a hill, I lived on a farm outside of Bakersfield.

A few of my friends would come out here and round up about a hundred or so of them. We would sell the snakes to local farmer and people that had gardens in town. There is nothing like a garter snake to keep down the bugs. If they are big enough they will keep care of the little mice too! The way we looked at it we were saving their lives.

We learn early to take them from the back of the group. If you try to take them from any other sections, they go nuts. They will attack and even rise up on their belly, their warming you to get away. Nice thing is they are not poisonous; they hurt a little when they bite, but nothing too bad.

We spent an hour or so just watching the snakes. Dennis showed the kids how to pick them up. To our surprise Enola and Treva had no problem picking them up. Dennis told us; yea we have snakes in our backyard at home. They are used to handling snakes!

There were so many different colors and different designs on them. Everyone was in awe; the grandkids were having fun playing with them. Thanks to Dennis for telling us all about them.

Dennis and Twila were going to stay in Bakersfield for a couple of days and meet up with us in Tucson, AZ. We're going to stay in Vegas for two days. Dennis showed us a great place to park the rigs for the night. It was an old school friend of his; it was a whole new side of Dennis we don't see very much. He was laughing talking about all the things they got in trouble for. There isn't anything like going back to your teenage years.

The evening was fun; we got to ride horses and help bring the cattle in for the night. We helped feed and milk the cows too. The grandkid knew how to milk them, because of their grandpa earlier this trip, showed them how to do it.

CHAPTER 18

Day 17
Las Vegas, NV

It was such a pretty night out, we all slept outside under the stars. It has been a long time since we slept under the night sky. It was so dark out; we could see all the stars. As we laid there talking, one at a time someone would fall asleep. Before too long, I was waking up to the sunrise.

Except for Twila and her family we all headed to Las Vegas. It should have taken us five hours, maybe six hours if we stopped for lunch. But it took us a lot longer. We were traveling along on Highway 101 when we got hung up behind a string of cars. We could see some red flashing lights in the distance. The guys, Frank, Frankie and James got out of their vehicles to see if they could find out what was holding up the traffic. They walked past other people who were standing outside of their cars. It was just too hot to be inside the cars. No one seemed to know what the problem was.

It was sometime before Frank and Frankie came back to tell us what the trouble was. He told us an old pickup loaded with chickens had a flat tire. It caused the pickup to swerve off the road and tipped over on its side. The driver is alright, he looked like he was pretty shaken up. I think he must be a local farmer. The officers were concerned because of his age in the beginning, but he looked like he was taking it quiet well.

A lot of people are trying to help him catch some of the chickens that had gotten out of their cages. We asked him where is James? Frank smiled and said, "He is trying to help catch the chickens." Then he started to laugh so hard he could hardly talk. He did manage to tell us they were loading some of the cages into the ambulance to get them off the highway.

I asked Frank you didn't want to help? Frank was still laughing and said "No Way." I asked him, what is so funny? Frankie spoke up, and in between their laughing they told us. There are about ten people running around trying to catch the chickens. They are bending over, with their hands out yelling here chick, here chick. They're not watching where they're going, so a couple of them had run into each other. A few have fallen or ran into rocks and hurt their foot. It's just chaos, but fun to watch.

Frank finally stops laughing long enough to say, "Remember how hard it was catching wild chickens, when we were stranded on Rosland Island. Well it was like that but worse. I had to laugh a little myself; I could only picture how funny Frank looked on the island. I could only imagine how ten people would look. I told them well I'm relieved that the farmer was not hurt.

When James came back he had more to tell us. There are a lot of people trying to help. The Sheriff said it would be another hour before the tow truck would arrive. So some of us guys got together and got the pickup right side up. We even got it started while someone fixed the flat tire. I think the old man felt like doing a jig. They have almost all the chickens loaded back in the truck even the ones in the ambulance. The Medics weren't too happy about cleaning out the ambulance. James was very pleased with himself, to be able to help someone in trouble. Maria came over and gave him a big hug and said, "My Hero!" He smiled and gave her a big kiss.

James said "It won't be long now till we can get going." He headed back to the others to let them know what happened. By the time we passed the spot where the pickup had turned over, all you could see is feathers. In an hour, no one will know there was an accident there.

We drove along about ten more miles and spotted a chicken farm. It was along side of the highway, we slowed down and there was the old farmer unloading his chickens. Frank tooted the horn and waved at him. He turned and waved back. James was hanging out of his window and tooted his horn and waved. We could actually see the old guy smiling and waving back. How good it was to know people still helped one another.

The rest of the way to Las Vegas went without any problems. Frank and I wanted to check out the new hotel we had heard about from Linda. She said it was really nice. It has been a very long time since we have been to Las Vegas. It might be fun to do a little gambling.

Our family didn't feel right about taking the kids into town. They felt there were just too many people. There was plenty for them to do at the camp ground; there was a rec. room with a pool table, ping pong table and two pools, one with a water slide. The only two that wanted to go with us was Maria and James. It was their first time in Vegas. They really wanted to do some gambling. The girls said they would watch the kids for them, so it was settled.

Frank and I wanted to spend the night in the hotel if we could get a room. It would be a nice change. We got settled at the campground which was really nice. I was surprised to see a slot machine in the office. I thought of course, this is Las Vegas!

The four of us headed to the hotel that Linda had told us about. James and Maria went right to the casino. Frank and I went over to the front desk to see if we could get a room. There was no problem; we got a room on the third floor.

We entered the elevator and to my hoarer it started to shift from side to side as we went up. We did make it to the third floor and quickly got out. I said I'm not doing that again. As we walked down the hallway Frank said "The first thing I'm going to do is call the desk! I can't believe they don't know about this." When we entered the room, we both caught our breath. It was so awesome, it even had a stocked bar. Frank made his call to inform them about the elevator. They said they would get right on it. While Frank was making his call I went to the restroom. When I flushed the toilet, to my surprise it filled with hot water. I called to Frank, come see this! Frank said, "I guess I'll make another call." I told him, wait until I take a shower. I wanted a shower that was big enough to turn around in and I didn't have to worry about how much water it took. Even better I didn't have to share the room with anyone else. It was wonderful!

Frank said "While the hotel is taking care of the problem, let's go find Maria and James." I'm ready to go, but let's take the stairs. Amen to that honey! Frank said.

As we went down the stairs we saw a crowd of people around the crap table. We squeezed in between the excited people, up closer to the table. There was Maria getting ready to throw the dice. She had James blow on her dice then let them go. Everyone was cheering! James and Maria were jumping up and down, they hugged each other. They decided to quite while they were ahead.

They spotted us and came over and gave us a hug. Maria was so excited she was breathless. James told us with a big grin on his face "Maria just won five thousand dollars!!!" When Maria finally got her voice she said "You know what were going to do? We're going to rent the banquet room and have the whole family for dinner." I told her that sounded wonderful!

I told the kids "Why don't you kids make arrangements for the dinner, while dad and I try out our luck at gambling. You can use our room if you need too, its room 324. I handed her my key, Frank still had his. Watch out if you use the elevator." We headed out for some fun. Frank said "Aren't you going to tell them about the water?" They can handle it, and then we laughed. It has been years since Frank and I have done any gambling. I thought I would try out the slot machines first. Frank went over to the crap table to play.

I just settled in at this one machine that looked lucky. I had my quarters ready, I put one in and was ready to pull the handle. This heavy looking woman came up and poked me in the ribs.

She hollered at me "'Git off my machine, this one is mine." I told her there are lots of other machines. I just put my money in this one. You can have it when I'm done. She was not listening to me. She started pushing me off of the stool. It made me angry, I push back but she was too big. She pulled my hair trying to pull me off the stool. Before I hit the floor, I grabbed her hair that was piled high on her head.

The next thing I knew we were struggling around on the floor. Then the security guys showed up and tried to pull us apart. I heard one of them say "Come on Maize, what have you been told about this kind of behavior?" They took her away while she was still arguing with them. I was thinking why me! I yelled at them, my money is in the machine and I am going to play it out! I was shaking as I climbed back on the stool. I started cranking the handle like crazy.

I didn't care if people were staring at me. Things settled down, I kept playing with a vengeance. I couldn't believe what happened next. The machine went crazy; coins started pouring out of the slot. I filled up the cup the cashier gave me! It kept pouring out of the machine. I had to start filling up my purse, then my pockets. Finally the machine stopped. I hurried over to the cashier and gave them all the coins, come to found out I had won $500.00. It really took away the excitement when that bitch gave me a hard time. I guess I did take her seat but she didn't need to be so nasty.

I went looking for Frank; he was still at the crap table. With a stern look on my face I told him come on Frank; I need to talk to you! He gathered up his chips and we headed toward the cashier. On the way I told him what had happened. I started shaking again. I felt tears coming into my eyes. I told him I didn't know what had come over me. She wasn't a bit polite, she was so mean! Frank put his arm around me, and said "Let me get these chips cashed in, then we'll go find the kids." When he was done cashing in his chips, he had won $800.00 dollars. I asked him if he enjoyed himself. He told me "Not really but the money helps."

We thought we had better go find the kids and see if everything was ready for the banquet. When we got to the banquet room, the whole family was there waiting for us. It was wonderful, the food was great! We had steak with all the trimming. Of course the grandkids had hamburgers with milk shakes. I didn't tell them what had happened to me, I didn't want to spoil the great dinner. After dinner we all talked awhile and had a few laughs. It was getting late so we all decided to call it a night.

Frank and I headed for the elevator which had an out of order sign on it. We sure didn't feel like going up three flights of stairs, but we found another one just around the corner. It was so great to get to our room. We relaxed for a while and had a drink from the bar. I turned on the radio. We decided to have a dance and found out we weren't so tired after all. We had a really great night. Especially when the hotel had sent some champagne, flowers, and an apology for what happened at the slot machines.

It was great waking up to a room where you could walk around in, and use the bathroom without waiting for someone to get out of. Don't get me wrong this vacation has been wonderful. But sometimes you just need your space. After we had a free breakfast we headed back to the campground. Everyone was packed up and ready to get back on the road.

CHAPTER 19

Day 19
Tucson, AZ

We arrived in Tucson late afternoon; it was in the 100's. Frank said "The K. O. A. camp is just ahead. Call the kids on the Walkie talkie and let them know." We weren't sure if they were watching the map or not. Three of the grandkids were riding with us in Seamore, the RV. As we pulled in we must have looked liked a caravan. It didn't take long for all the grandkids to get out and head for the playground, while we checked in. It seemed like no time at all to get camp set up. We all had a routine to get everything ready to settle in.

Twila and Dennis had already arrived at the campsite. They were all settled in and had reserved the spaces around them for us. I asked them how it all went, they said great. Dennis said, "It was nice to visit with family and friends. We went on a snake round up and just hung out at my friend's farm." I asked Dennis what kind of snakes, he said rattlesnakes. If we don't keep them under control they eat the garter snakes.

Twila isn't much for keeping a journal, when we had a little time to talk she said it was great fun. They went to a rodeo and went to a country night club and danced the night away.

Everyone but me headed up to the Main building to check things out. I wanted to take a well needed shower. So I took my robe and bath towel and headed out to find the shower place. The showers were in the back part of the facility. I figured it would save on our supply of water in Seamore. The showers had to be bigger than the one in the Seamore. It was so nice taking my time in a hot shower. No doubt the others will want to clean up soon. Twenty minutes later I was getting dried off. The rest of the gang was starting to come in. I decided to dress in the R.V.

I put my robe on and wrapped the towel around my head. There were some amused looks, as I walked by the other rigs. When I got back to Seamore, to my surprise it was locked! I thought I would wait for Frank to come back, instead of trying to find him. I sat down at a nearby picnic table, I sat there gazing about. It was a really nice place. Very few trees but was very nicely landscaped. I sat there watching the little creature of the desert, lizards, birds and squirrels.

A few strangers passed by and hardly noticed me. As I sat there my ankles started to itch. I only had on my rubber thongs. I looked down and to my shock there was an ant hole right next to my feet. I jumped up and then I noticed I was in the wrong parking space. As I was hurrying away, I was shaking my feet to get the ants off me.

Ok, this is not a good idea. I'm going to go find Frank and get the keys. I headed to the main building, as I entered I saw Frank at a small eating area, he was sitting at table, at the far end of the building. I noticed everyone was dressed except me.

I went up to Frank and taped him on the shoulder and asked him for the keys. He just looked up and said "Sure honey." I fished them out of his pocket. He continued to talk to an old lady that was sitting with him. He didn't even notice that I was standing there in my robe. I was starting to get angry because of his lack of attention. I took the keys and hurried back to Seamore, as fast as I could.

The damn key doesn't fit! Which one is it, anger started to well up inside me and I gave the Seamore a kick! Needless to say I hurt my toe. As I was jumping around the towel fell off my head and the tie on my robe was coming loose. I guess the passer byes had a good laugh. After taking a deep breath I settled down. I found the right key, thank goodness. Finally, I was in Seamore and I could get dressed. I got dressed in my jeans and sweat shirt; I put my hair up in a pony tail.

I was feeling much better after I got dressed. I went back to the Main building to join Frank. That is if he isn't too busy talking to someone. In spite of my sore toe and my itchy ankles, I waved at the kids who were busy around their trailers. I thought maybe Frank did have the right idea about talking to fellow travelers. I thought maybe I'll give it a try, if I get the chance. When I entered the building our granddaughters, Sharlene and Enola was sitting with Frank. The old lady was gone that he was talking too earlier.

I spotted the grocery part of the store. Maybe they would have some salve for my ankles. As I was buying some salve I spotted this lady over by a magazine rack. I thought here is my chance to start a conversation with a stranger. I went over to her and said very cheerfully "This is quite a nice camping area isn't it?" She turned around and looked up and down at me and literally stuck her nose up in the air. Then she walked away and left me there with a very embarrassed look on my face.

I thought so much for that. I guess Frank has a better technique. When I joined Frank and the grandkids Frank asked me if I was all right, I just said I'm fine very calmly. I asked him, what have they got to eat? He answered "Great hamburgers". I replied "Guess that's what I'll have, I ordered the biggest one they have and some French fries."

The girls got up and gave me a hug. They had finished and were anxious to go run around. After they left, Frank looked me square in the eyes and said "Alright Aggie what is bothering you? Oh, nothing really, I'll be fine once I eat. Go get us our food." I thought what's the point of complaining is. It wasn't his fault I got locked out of Seamore.

Everyone stayed at their own places tonight. We planned on all going to the movie later on; it was going to be outside. They were having it at the campground, in the park. It was bring your own chairs and popcorn. I decided not to go but I heard it was a really good movie. I stayed at home and read a book. It's been a long time since I did that. It was a nice change.

When Frank came in he told me everyone was asking if I was ok. I told them you just needed some down time for yourself. I thanked him and went back to reading my book. Frank crawled into bed and he was asleep in no time. I wasn't far behind him, reading did the trick.

CHAPTER 20

Day 20
Deming, NM

We left pretty early from Tucson; we wanted to do some rock hounding in Deming, NM. We stopped in a place called Shakespeare Ghost Town on our way to Deming. "In 1870, a silver strike caused Shakespeare, once a small settlement on the stage line to California, to grow into a town named Ralston with a population of around 3,000." The good news is we didn't see or meet any ghosts this time.

We arrived around noon in Deming, and set up camp and had lunch. They had beautiful rocks all around the parking area by the Main building. I'm not sure what types of mineral they were. The host said most were found in this area, the rest came from Nevada.

After lunch, we headed to the City of the Rocks State Park, according to the sign at the entry way. "The City of the Rocks was created 34.9 million years ago by a volcanic eruption. Then over millions of years, erosion sculpted the different rock formations." To me it looks like giants used to live there. There were huge rocks that look like chairs, one that looked like a bed. The City of the Rocks just sits out in the middle of the desert.

"The Mimbreno Indians settled in the area about 750 - 1250 AD. Pottery, arrowheads, and other artifacts show evidence of prehistoric Indians in the area. Indian wells, or conical holes, are found in the rocks where water would be allowed to collect." This information came from the flyer. It is amazing how many places we have visited during this trip that was settled by Indians first.

We let the kids go play on the rocks. Frankie yelled at them to be careful, we don't need any broken bones. It looked like Daniel and Douglas found some friends. I could see them sitting on top of a rock with two girls. I pointed it out to Wanda, all she could say was, "Oh no, I hope this doesn't mean they are starting to like girls. I was hoping for at least a couple more years."

It was so nice there, but we had an appointment to go rock hounding. We wanted to wait until it cooled off a little bit before we went. We called everyone in and loaded up the cars.

It didn't take us long to get to the site. The site owner was there waiting for us. "We'll be looking for thunder eggs and perlite; it is a shiny black glassy rock," he told us.

It was a little more work but we did find some nice stones. After digging around for about two hours, we gave up and headed back to camp. We found some nice stones, but nothing like we found at my folk's place.

The guys said they would do the cooking tonight. What a great surprise, next thing I knew a pizza delivery truck came up to us. The guys all yelled "Dinners ready!" But to be fair they did make a salad. It was nice; we hadn't had pizza in awhile. We talked about our trip so far, and what part everyone liked so far. Visiting my family of course!

CHAPTER 21

El Paso, TX - Ft. Bliss
Day 21 and 22

We were stationed here when our kids were 10, 12, and 14, just starting their teens. We lived in military housing in the beginning, it was nice. It was great for the kids, because there were kids everywhere to play with. We wanted a home to call our own. We ended up buying a brand new home. We picked out the carpet and the color of the walls. It was fun to watch it get built. It was a four bedroom, two full baths, and a big yard. It was more space than we ever had before. The kids each had their own room and each could get their own dog. We did have to plant grass and trees, that's something that the desert doesn't have. We were at the city limit, so everything behind us was desert, when we first moved in. By the time we left, there was a new highway and the city limit was five miles past our house.

The kids wanted to see where we use to live at. It really hasn't change that much. When we lived there it looked like a new neighborhood, now it looked like an old one. It's interesting how neighborhoods ages with time, it's hard to explain but when the neighborhood is new everything looks new, as the neighborhood ages, the trees get bigger, there is less grass, no basketball nets on the garages. There were always kids in the street playing now, you don't see anyone. Kind of sad, I think.

We had set up camp at the campground outside of town. When we got back we went for a walk, and before you know it Frankie, Daniel and Douglas, was finding lizards, horny toads and even a tarantula under a rock. Wanda kept telling the boys to be careful, and put them back. It was funny to watch, because we did the same thing with our kids. Both Twila and Maria were both tomboys, Frankie and the girls would go out with their friends and play war. We made it a rule early on that they couldn't bring anything home. The other rule was don't kill anything, and put the creature back where you found it.

When we lived here in El Paso, Frank was station at Ft. Bliss. We could see the Franklin Mountain from our house. We spend a lot of time in the desert; funny thing is we never ran into a rattlesnake. We had heard that there was a lost mine somewhere on the mountain. So we would take the kids out and see if we could find it. Needless to say we never did find it. Frankie has the bug, and so does his family. They have been doing some research about the mine. Frankie and Wanda were going to take their boys, Daniel and Douglas, out looking for the mine, just like we used to do. While they were out looking, the rest of us went over to our friend's house, and hung out at their pool. We had BBQ steaks and hot dogs for dinner. It was a nice evening, when we got back Frankie and his family wasn't back yet.

It was still early, so we all sat around and played cards. As it started to get dark we started getting a little worry. Frank told me their fine; they know how to keep care of themselves. But I could tell he was a little worried too. We decided to give them thirty more minutes than we would go look for them. They had told us where they would be parking their car and what trail they would be taking.

After thirty minutes they still had not returned, so Frank, Dennis and James headed up to the mountain to find them. I stayed behind just in case they showed up. I was going crazy, so was everyone else. After about an hour and a half, they all pulled into camp. We all ran over to them, there were hugs all around. Frankie didn't look to good, I asked him what happened. He told me, "Mom, give us a minute and we'll tell you what happened. I asked Tina to go get everyone some water, she ran off to get it. All the girls ran after, because they wanted to help too. While we waited, Frank told us they had found Wanda outside the cave; she was waiting for us to show up.

I couldn't stand it any longer, ok tell me what happened. Frankie asked Wanda, why you don't tell them. I could tell Frankie was still in a lot of pain. Wanda smiled and kissed Frankie on the forehead and said sure. This is their story; I did add a little history to it.

Frankie and Wanda story

We took the boys to Hucco Tanks, which is an oasis in the middle of the dry land all around us. It is also said to have spiritual power, an area favored by the gods of the mountains and the desert. It was used in ceremonies to celebrate the miracle of rain. There are petroglyphs and painted pictographs all through the rocks and cave of Hucco Tanks. Douglas spoke up and said, "The painting were of hunters and gatherers and some Indians with mask. Dad said they were known as the Jornada Branch of the Mogollon. There was also Apache and Kiowa living here at one time. The painting were everywhere, it was so cool. Daniel agreed with his brother, and said we even found a small cave."

Wanda continues, "After showing our boys Hucco Tanks area, Frankie started talking about the lost mines. As you know Frankie has been researching the histories of the mines for years. Once the boys said, "Let's go looking for the mine, we all went looking for the mines, as you all know. Daniel and Douglas were in the lead, when Douglas saw a rabbit go into a hole. They both went over to check it out. I told them to be careful, jack rabbits are not the friendliest of rabbits. All I got was yea, yea!

We were all around the hole; Daniel had pulled some rocks out. He said, "There is a bigger opening behind the rocks. Frankie shone a light in the hole, about that time the jacket rabbit come flying out of the hole. It scared the hell out of us. You would have thought it had been a rattlesnake. But it didn't take long for the guys to start digging.

After awhile the hole was big enough for Douglas to get into. He took his Dad's flashlight and crawled into the dark. I

131

love having boys; otherwise I know Frankie would have had to crawl into the hole. Douglas called out; it looks like a mine or some kind of cave. I can't see the back of it. Frankie told him to come back out. As we waited for him to come out, he didn't show, his Dad yelled at him again. Next thing Douglas's head popped out, with a smile, Surprise! It scared the hell out of us again. I told him don't do that, than we all laughed. Douglas said he was waiting for them to get close to the opening so he could scare them. Douglas does like to surprise people.

Douglas climbed out of the hole and we started pulling the rocks away from the entrance way. We were very careful; we didn't want the rocks to collapse on us. We made the hole about three feet around, and we crawled in, one at a time.

Frankie said it is an old mine, we had all four flashlights on. But Frankie told us to turn two of them off. Just in case their battery died. The man is always thinking. Wanda smiled at him and patted him on his leg a little too hard; he gave out a little yelp. She apologized to him and continued with their story.

We must have walked a good half mile into the mine. Every once in a while we would hear something. Frankie said, "It's just the mountain talking to us." After awhile, Daniel came up to me and said, "Mom, I feel like someone is watching us." I had to agree with him, the farther we went into the mine, and the weirder it felt. All we found so far was an old sack and some mining tools. Which was strange, wouldn't the miner take their tools. I kept telling Frankie, we need to turn back, but he kept saying just a little farther. Frankie spoke up in his defense, "The mine was safe, and so I figured why not go as far as we could. Wanda said, "Anyway!" Wanda continued.

It felt like we had walked miles, when Frankie felt cold air. He said, "There must be an opening around here." Just then both of the flashlights went out. We were so glad that we had turned off the other two. We also had extra batteries in our backpacks. We could see a light down in the mine, it wasn't very big. It looked like it was moving around; we all looked at each other. Daniel asked, "Dad what is that?" Frankie told him, he didn't have a clue. Let's go check it out. The boys took the lead; I was more than willing to hang back.

As we got closer to the light, it got colder, this didn't make any sense. If we were getting closer to an opening, it should be getting warmer. I began to think this wasn't a good idea. We should have reached the light by now. I grabbed Frankie by the arm and told him we need to turn around. It was strange, it was like he was in a trance and I woke him. It took him a couple of second, and then he yelled at the boys to come back. They had continued to walk towards the light. They didn't stop, so Frankie ran up to them, and shook their arms. They acted the same way as Frankie did. It was a good thing, it didn't affect me.

We stood there for a few minutes, trying to figure out what was going on. We started hearing noises coming down the mine. We all agreed it was time to get out of there. As we started heading back to the original opening, we continued to hear noise, and it was getting really cold.

That's when it happened! The mine started shaking, and the rocks started falling and that's when a pile of rocks collapsed around Frankie. He was behind us; at this point we were all running. Then we heard Frankie yell, and we turned and he was lying on the ground.

We ran back to him, that's when we saw a black shadow on the mine wall. Douglas stopped, "Mom do you see the shadow, I told him yes. But we need to help your father get out of here. We started removing the rocks off his leg. It looked like he was ok, there was no blood and I didn't see any bones sticking out. Frankie smiled and said "Nice Wanda!" As he stood up, he scream in pain, I guess he hurt his leg worse than we thought. Anyway, we helped him get up, Douglas was watching the shadow, and it just stood there, like it was watching us.

We tried to carry Frank out, but we had gone a lot farther than we thought. We had to stop and take a break. The boys and I just didn't have the strength to carry him any farther. As soon as the rocks had fallen on Frankie, the mine stopped shaking. I told Frankie, I'm going for help. He told me to take Doug, but don't go too far from the mine opening. People have lost mine openings before. My family should be looking for us. They know where we would be going. So use the walkie talkie, and keep calling to them. I didn't like leaving him behind, but we didn't know how much farther we had to go, and he was in a lot of pain. I'm pretty sure we weren't helping.

Douglas and I took off, at a slow run; we didn't have any idea how far we would have to go. To our surprise, we really went in a long ways into the mine. When we finally got to the opening it was already dark. Frankie's family had to be looking for us. I turned on the walkie talkie, and started calling for help. I didn't hear anything for about ten minutes, and then Frank's voice came over the walkie talkie. All I could say is Thank God it's you!" I told him what path we had taken. He asked me what was wrong, I told him Frankie hurt his leg and he can't walk.

He's in the mine Daniel is with him. I'm pretty sure he'll have to be carried out.

I have never been so happy to see the three guys coming up the hill. I pointed to the mine, and Douglas told them, I'll show you where Dad and Daniel are. Frank told him lead the way, they all disappeared into the mine. I just sat on a rock and waited for them to come back out. I really didn't what to see the dark shadow again, or anything else to do with the mine. I knew the guys would get my husband and son out of there.

Pretty soon, they came out of the mine. They had done a king chair to carry Frank out. It was hard to get him out of the mine, because of the small hole but Frankie crawled out. I could tell he was in a lot of pain.

Frank had checked his leg before he moved him, and told me it wasn't broken, but damn near. Once we got Frankie out, we let him rest for a little bit, and then carried him down the path. They did the king chair as much as they could, but there was parts where Frankie had to hop on one leg. James had found a stick for Frankie to use as a cane.

I didn't think we would ever get back to the car. It was wonderful to see it. Frank asked Frankie, do you want to go to the hospital. Frankie said no, so here we are safe and sound!

I could tell Wanda wasn't too happy with Frankie decision. We had Frankie take off his pants, so I could look at it. It was pretty bruised, and I couldn't find any broken bones. We gave him two aspirin and put a cold compress on his leg. But his leg still hurt, but it was doing better. I had Wanda put some oils I had on his leg, it stopped most of the pain for awhile anyway. The rest of the night he was waited on hand and foot.

I asked Wanda and Frankie, what do you think the dark shadow was? Without missing a beat, Frankie said, "It was probably a spirit from one of the miner that used to work or died in the mine. Wanda said, "I don't know, but it had all the guys in a trance. I don't know why it didn't affect me, but I'm sure glad it didn't. We would have never been found.

What a night, we ended up telling ghost stories and enjoying the summer evening in El Paso. Tomorrow we're going on post and getting some supply. The plan was to head out tomorrow, but Frankie needs to take it easy for a day.

Day 22

Frank and I got up earlier than the rest, so we sat outside and had our coffee and watched the sun come up. It was beautiful! It was still all around us. As we drank our coffee we talked about a little of everything. Then the subject of Frankie and his family came up. How close we came to losing them.

I told Frank I could only imagine how the kids felt when we came up missing. As I waited here wondering what had happened to them. I thought I was done going exploring. Everything in me wanted to go with you guys and help find them. I knew I needed to stay here with the grandkids. Every car, every noise I would jump up, in hopes it was them. Frank said he knew how I felt. Every turn, every road he would look down, to make sure they wouldn't be there. All I knew is we needed to find them. All the way there, not a word was spoken between the three of us. I think we were afraid what we might find.

When we heard Wanda over the walkie talkie, my heart started double timing it. The first thing I asked her is everyone ok. That second took forever to hear her response. When she said yes, I haven't felt that happy since we returned from the Rosland Island.

Then she said "Frankie is hurt and inside of the mine. All I knew is we had to help him. Dennis and James took the lead, when the path split James took one and Dennis and I took the other. Lucky the path joined up after a little bit. They were really out there, I'm just glad we had them take the walkie talkie with them.

When we saw Wanda, James started yelling and waving at her. I don't think I have ever seen James get that excised before. Both Dennis and James took off like a rocket. I wasn't far behind I was really feeling my age. But once I saw Wanda, I felt thirty again.

Wanda was in tears, but she didn't start crying until she saw us. I think it was the relief of seeing us, she couldn't help it. She told us what happened, and pointed at the hole. Douglas was pretty upset, but he took charge and told us, come on I'll show you where they are. We asked Wanda to stay out, just in case and she agreed. I really don't think she wanted to go back in anyway. As we were going in, she grabbed my arm and said "There is something weird in there, be careful! I didn't understand, but I told her I will.

They were pretty far in there, which I don't understand. Frankie knows better than to go that deep into a mine, especially with his family with him. He didn't have the equipment he would need either.

When we reached them, Daniel had his Dad's head on his lap. They only had the one flashlight; the other one had gone out. I can only imagine how scared he was. It was almost black in there, if it wasn't for his flashlight, it would have been pitch black. Frankie had passed out, I guess from the pain. Daniel waited for us to help his Dad, and kept telling us to be careful with him. Frankie woke up once we started lifting him. He was very confused, I told Daniel to take the lead with me. James and Dennis made a kings chair, and carried Frankie that way until we arrived at the entrance hole. The trick was to get Frankie through the small hole and not hurt him.

As you heard from Wanda, that didn't happen. I had Daniel, Douglas and Dennis go out. James and I pushed Frankie through the hole, while Daniel and Dennis pulled him through the hole. It broke my heart to hear Frankie yell out in pain.

The rest of the story you know from Wanda.

As I looked at Frank, I could see tears in his eyes. I knew how he felt. I can't image the idea of losing Frankie and his family and never knowing what happened to them. God was looking over them and us that day.

Day 23

Everyone was starting to get up; I kissed Frank and told him I'll get him another cup of coffee. He smiled at me with his wonderful smile, and everything was all right again.

When I came back out with the coffee, there was Frankie and Wanda. First thing that came out of Frankie mouth was, "Where's my coffee?" I laughed and said it's in Seamore go get it for yourself. Frankie replied, "Well I guess the spoiling me is over." Wanda gave him a kiss, and told him not yet I'll get it for you. We all laughed and before too long everyone were there.

Maria said, "So what's the plan for today?"

I told her that Dad and I are going to Ft. Bliss to check it out and go to the PX and the commissary to pick up a few things. We might stop at the museum and look around. Anyone that wants to come is welcome.

Funny we didn't have any takers. Dennis and Twila told us they wanted to go to Juarez, Mexico and pick up some pots for her plants. Maria and James asked if they could go with them. Twila said, "Sure sis, it would be more fun with you along anyway." Dennis looked at Twila and said "Hey!" She smiled and said, "Just kidding," and then she winked at Maria.

Frankie said, "I'm going to hang out here." He suggested to Wanda, why don't you and the boys go? Wanda and the boys all said, "No, we had enough excitement yesterday. We'll hang out here and go to the pool."

It didn't take long for everyone to disappear. We headed to Ft. Bliss, which was only a hop, skip and a jump from here. We went by the museum, nothing had changed. We went to the PX (it is a military department store) Frank wanted to pick up a couple of military things from the clothing store. Then we ended up at the commissary (which is a grocery store, just in case you didn't know). We wanted steaks and potatoes for dinner.

We got everything done, and headed home. Frankie and family were at the pool, and the others hadn't returned from Mexico yet. I started to worry, and Frank said, "Stop worrying, it still early, they will be fine!" I told him to stop reading my mine!

Let's go join Frankie and his family at the pool, Frank suggested. That sounds good to me, so we changed and went to the pool. It was nice sitting around, lying out in the sun and visiting with the kids. Daniel and Douglas swim like Merbeings; they can do three lapses underwater. I'm pretty sure they could swim more lapses if they wanted too.

Grandpa had a surprise for Daniel and Douglas; he had purchased them a set of fatigues. He had purchased them at the military clothing store, on post. The boys had told him earlier that they would love to have a set of fatigues. They wanted a set, so they could go play out in the desert with their friends. That's all it took for Grandpa to buy them a set.

After waiting a little while, he called the boys over to give them their gift. Frankie and Wanda had already known that we were going to get them the Army uniform for the boys. They both had big smiles on their faces, as they waited to see the boy's expression. It didn't take long for them to react once they saw the military bag. They knew what they had gotten. They each grabbed their bags and started digging through it. You think it was Christmas or something. Frank even got them the green socks the soldiers would wear with the uniform.

They turned to their folks, and asked if it was okay if they go change and go play in the desert with their friends. They said yes, and Frankie told them to take a walkie talkie with them, just in case and bring them the other one. Daniel agreed and they both ran off to the tent to change into their uniforms. When they came out of the tent, they looked like little soldiers from top to bottom. Grandpa not only bought them the fatigues, but he bought them the hat and boots to go with the uniform. One thing about Grandpa, he loves to make his grandkids happy.

They came over and handed the walkie-talkie to Frankie and ran off to find their friends. Wanda yelled at them, "You be back by 6 o'clock!" Douglas waved his hand and said, "We will" and then they were gone. Frankie turned to his dad and told him, "You got a little carried away didn't you dad?" Frank just smiled and said "Not really," it could have been worse I could of gotten them class A's uniform, too. We all laughed, and laid around the pool a little while.

I kept looking at my watch to see what time it was. I was wondering when the girls would get back, when all of a sudden we heard a horn honking. I turned to see who it was. The girls were finally home, we were still at the swimming pool with Frankie and Wanda. As they drove by, we waved at them. They had taken Frankie's van so they could all ride together. I was so glad to see them back! I'm becoming quite the worrywart these days.

Sharlene and Enola came running over yelling, "Grandma, Aunt Wanda, come see all the things we got in Mexico." They grabbed our hands and started pulling us towards the van. "Come on," she was yelling at us. Wanda said "okay, okay, were moving as fast as we can!"

When we arrived at the van, it looked like they had bought everything they could find in Mexico. The girls pulled out their brand-new dresses they had gotten there. They were beautiful. I'm not sure why they had to have them, but they were happy and that's all that matters! There were all kinds of pots for plants, piggy banks of all sorts: little monkeys and dogs with big eyes. They even had decoration that you hang from the ceiling. They even had a few Christmas looking decorations. James pulled out a wooden shield with swords crossing in the middle of it, and to other pieces that had candleholders on them. The background was in red velvet, with other decorations on them. They were cool looking! I asked him where he was going to hang them, and he told me above the fireplace. We're going to put my families crest in the middle of the black. Dennis piped up and said, I wanted one, but Twila told me No, he was pouting like a little boy. Then he said, but she was right. We really don't have any place to put it!

The next thing I know Twila was telling on Maria. She told me, they were shopping in the open mall. They had gotten separated and Maria started yelling out, "Twila, come check out something she had found." Twila started heading towards Maria, when all of the vendors started calling her name. "Twila, Hey Twila, come check this out, as she walked by each of the vendors they had to say something to her. They would call her name and ask her to come by check out this. The whole time Maria and the kids were laughing at me. Mom! Maria said, "I didn't do it on purpose Mom." I told Maria. I'm sure you didn't do it on purpose sweetheart! Then we all started laughing, I miss my little girls sometimes!

The rest of the evening we enjoyed the warm evening. Daniel and Douglas came back from their adventure in the desert and were telling us about all the different things that they found. They had found a tarantula, scorpion, and Horney toad. Douglas said "We did hear a rattlesnake but we backed off and went a different direction. He turned to his dad and said just like you told us, Dad!" Frankie told him "Good job!"

The steaks were wonderful; Dennis had picked up a sauce from the restaurant, they had eaten at in Mexico. We used sauce to cook the steaks. Later we had s'mores and played board games and pinochle. Tomorrow we will be heading towards San Antonio; there is the cavern that is called the caverns of Sedona that were going to stop at. It's hard to believe that we have been on the road for 23 days.

As much as I have enjoyed seeing all the wonderful things, the United States has to offer. It's hard to believe we have only seen a small part of it, there is so much more to see. Frank and I have been talking about getting a trailer and do more traveling before we get too old.

CHAPTER 22

Day 24
Caverns of Sonora

The cavern is located outside of Sonora, Texas; it took us a little over six hours to get here. The Mayfield family owned the land where the cavern was found. It is a funny story how they found the cavern. They were out with their dog. When the dog took chase after a raccoon, the raccoon ran into a 20 inch opening and the dog followed the raccoon into the hole. When they went after the dog, they discover it went back at least 500 feet. In the early 20's, the locals began exploring the caves. After about 500 feet from the entrance, there was a 50 foot deep pit. Needless to say, they couldn't see down to the bottom of it. In 1956, Jack Burch, a caver from Oklahoma saw the cavern for the first time. He saw what human impact was doing to the cavern; there was damage wherever there was human interaction. In 1959, his vision came to be. They started the development of the Caverns of Sonora; by 1960 the caverns were open to the public.

We arrived at the caverns around 3 o'clock. We set up camp, they had a campground right there on their property so it was easy access to all of the things we wanted to do. It only had power and water at the site, there was no septic but that would be okay. It was still early enough so all of us could park next to each other. After we had dinner, we headed up to the Lodge. It had a little store and lots of animal heads on the wall. It looked like it was a pretty old building.

As we were in the store, we looked out the window and we could see storm clouds coming straight at us. So we decided we wanted to get back to the trailer before it arrived. The trailers weren't that far from the Lodge probably about 100 yards or so. The storm was really moving fast. We just got into Seymour when the rain hit, within minutes day light turned to night. We heard the lightning and then the thunder show started. It was funny all of us started counting when we saw the lightning we wanted to see how close the main storm was. So when the lightning did its thing, we all started counting one, two, and so on. We got up to 10 the first time. By the third lighting hit, the storm was right on top of us. The storm came rolling in; the clouds were black, with the lightning running for miles in the sky. As the rain poured down in sheets, we watched our own natural show. It lasted about an hour and then it was gone. It left as fast as it arrived.

It smelled so clean, and it was a kind of humid outside. We decided to go to Twila's trailer and play cards for a little while; it started to get late so we headed back to Seymour. As we were walking back, we noticed that there was a herd of deer grazing by the fence line, just hanging out in the field. They didn't seem to care one way or the other about us. There were a couple little babies hanging out with their moms.

Day 25
Cavern of Sonora

After everyone had their breakfast and coffee, we decided to go back up to the Lodge and see what they had there. They had a place in the back where you could pan for minerals. You buy a bag of sand and with minimal in it, from the store, and they guarantee there will be a variety of minerals in the bag. We went out to the back area where we could do the panning. They had little trays with screens on the bottom of them, and you wash them in the running water. It was called a sluice box; it was about twenty feet long. We had a great time there were woos and awes all around. We also had to compare who had the biggest stones. We found different types of quartz, amethyst, rubies and a few others that I'm not sure what they were. All I knew was they were pretty and cool looking. According to our granddaughters!

Our group was the first in line for the tour. In fact, we had the tour guide all to ourselves. That seemed to be the thing on each of the tours that we went on, go figure! I guess when you have fourteen people traveling together; it's a tour group in its self.

We walked down some stairs to the first cavern. It defiantly was a lot different than Inner Space Cavern; we had gone to earlier this year with the kids. As we were going into the cavern Treva grabbed my hand and reminded me not to touch anything because we didn't want to kill the rocks. I gave her a big hug and told her, thanks for reminding me. I guess she remembered about what happened at the inner space cavern.

We went deeper and deeper into the cavern; every room had something different to show us. It is amazing how beautiful it was under ground, with the lights behind the stone, they looked amber. As we walked into each of the different rooms, the stones would glow. Some looked like they were on fire, but most gave off this wonderful glow. It's hard to believe that you are so far underground and you feel right at home. Some people are scared of going underground. But I think if they ever tried this, they would forget their fear and enjoyed it tremendously.

As we followed the guide to though the caverns they were telling us the name of the different types of shapes and what they were called. Again, it is so amazing how many different shapes there are in these caverns. It was so quiet, no one was talking, except for a few woos and aahs. In the back ground you could hear water dripping onto the stones, and a small creek running slowing through the cavern. We were told it was the water coming through from above.

As we exited the cavern, the bright sunlight made us all squeak and cover our faces. It was definitely a lot warmer outside than it was in the caverns. I think she said it stays about 60° inside the cavern. We took off our jackets in a matter of minutes. It was 85 degrees outside.

We headed back to the campsite to have lunch. After lunch we decided to take a hiking trail that wasn't too far from our campsite. It was a wonderful walk; the nice thing was it was all flat. There was a lot of sage and other brush, but the trail was maintained. It took us about an hour and a half to do the loop. It's a good thing we took a lot of water with us. We have four military canteens and two western type canteens that we always carry with us when we go out hiking. It would have been great to have these on the Rosland Island, but we made do with what we had.

When we got back to camp, three other rigs had come into the camp ground. Frank and I enjoy checking out the different rigs people have and to see where they came from. As we walked by them, we would say Hi, and the rest of our clan would do the same. By the end of our clan line, I think everyone was done saying Hi back to us. There was a group fire pit, at the camp ground. The kids wanted to have a fire and roast marshmallow. We went up to the lodge and brought some wood. They told us we could also pick up the wood in the fields if we wanted too. We send the grandkids off to collect wood for the fire. They all came back with arms full of wood. For the little ones that would be three pieces. Daniel and Douglas had grabbed a towel and loaded it up with wood, and carried it back together. We were good for the whole night.

After dinner we went over to the fire pit and started the fire. We always had our sticks; we carried our marshmallow sticks with us. You never know when you may need them. It wasn't too long before other campers joined us at the fire pit. A couple of them had guitars and one had a banjo, they were good. Come to find out they were a band; they were called "The Rose Bud." They named their band after an old friend, which had pasted when they were younger. He had died at 22 in a car accident. Rick didn't tell us anything else about his friend that died. Just that it was a great loss to him and his friends.

Before too long, everyone was singing and dancing. I think everyone at the camp ground was there. It was great fun; we made new friends and exchanged address. Who knows if Frank and I decide to get a RV, we'll have someone to go visit. There were people from North Caroline, Florida, Montana, Wyoming and even Texas.

As the night went on people would get up and sing there was also a few sing along. It was pretty late by the time the fire was getting low; it was after midnight before we headed back to the RV. The grandkids went to the trailers around 10:00, and so did Twila. She said, "It was her turn to watch the kids. I think it was because she was tired and wanted to go to bed early for a change. Around 1:00, Frank and I said our good nights and thanked The Rose Bud, for the great music.

As we were walking back to Seamore, Frank asked, "Are you glad we went on this trip?" I turned and looked at him and said, I couldn't think of anything I loved more, than spending this time with our family. It gave us time to get to know them better. The good news we didn't kill each other! Frank laughed and said, "That's true, most family wouldn't last a week." Then he kissed me, and told me he loved me! The look in his eyes, I knew I couldn't love anyone more than him. I think someone is going to get lucky tonight!

CHAPTER 23

Day 26

Everyone was moving a little slow this morning. Frank was already up and had the coffee ready. As I walked into the front of Seamore, he handed me my cup of coffee, and gave me a kiss good morning. We both agreed it was a great night. I asked him if the kids are up yet, he said he hasn't seen any movement. He had already walked around the camp ground, and didn't see anyone accept Chad. He was one of the band members we met last night. Also, the herd of deer was back, he said it looked like there were twins in the herd.

We went outside and watched the camp ground come to life. First it was the people that had pets. Then the kids came out and headed to the play ground. Once our grandkids saw us sitting outside, they came running over, to say good morning.

I asked them if they had a good time. Enola said, "It was wonderful, I'm going to be a singer." Sharlene said, "Me too." Tina had to join in, "We can have a band like the Rose Buds!" They all agreed that it would be a great idea. Then Grandpa said, "Well I'll be your manager." They all laughed and headed back to the play ground, some of their new friends had come out to play.

Pretty soon the rest of the clan came out of their trailers. We all talked about last night and what great fun it was. We talked about our next stop either San Antonia or Austin. We wanted one more night out with the kids before we went home to Houston. The vote was in were going to San Antonia and going to the zoo, and the river walk.

It didn't take long to get to San Antonio, Texas. We set up camp, but this time we couldn't park next to each other. The campground was pretty full; I guess that's what happens when you travel on a weekend. But it wasn't a problem; they had a recreation building that we could all meet in, if we wanted to.

So our first stop was the zoo; we used to take our kids there when they were younger. Our kids have taken their kids here; they take them at least once a year. We all enjoy visiting the San Antonio zoo. They have made a lot of improvements through the years, in the beginning the animals were in small cages, but now they are in larger areas so they can move around better. Hopefully, in time, all the animals will have a better place to live. I can't even imagine not having any space to move around in.

The older grandkids rode on an elephant this time; the little ones were too small. But it won't be long, before they will be big enough, if they are still going to the zoo. The little ones were pretty upset about not being able to ride on the elephant; Maria took them to the monkey cages, which was their favorite anyway. That was their favorite place to go! We would join them after the kids were done riding the elephant. Funny thing is, before it was all over, all of us rode on the elephant's. It wasn't too bad; it was like riding in a chair that moved side to side. Basically, they put a little bench on top of the elephant and you sat in it. The elephant had a pad on it, to protect it from getting hurt, underneath the bench.

We were at the zoo for a couple of hours, it was great fun. We went to a Mexican restaurant on the River Walk. It was wonderful, there is nothing like Tex-Mex food. Tex-Mex food is a little bit of Mexican and a little bit of Texan mixed together. A little on the spicy side, but the flavor is wonderful. After we ate we went on a walk down the river.

Here's a little history about San Antonio, the "San Antonio River symbolizes the heart and soul of the city. Hundreds of years ago, the river was a gathering place for Native Americans. The first civilian Spanish settlers built their homes here in the 1700s. In the late 1920s, the San Antonio Conservation Society, local government officials and business leaders realized what an asset the river could be to the growing city. River Walk plans eventually was a 21-block section from Nueva to Lexington, completed in March of 1941, just in time for Fiesta. The project transformed downtown through beautification, preservation and flood control." The River Walk is one of our favorite things to do here. But the zoo is our favorite.

We were so full from dinner we decided to take the sightseeing boat, instead of walking. As usual we took over the whole boat; it was a great way to spend the afternoon.

We got back to the campground a little after 4 o'clock. We agreed to meet at Seymour in about an hour. It was hot out, but it was finally cooling off a little.

Frank and I grabbed a beer and sat out under the awning of Seymour, watching people go by. Sitting in the shade, helped out a lot. I told Frank if we started traveling in an RV, we will need to get a dog. It seems like everyone has a dog here.

Just like clockwork, everyone started showing up. We pointed to the ice chest, and told them the drinks are in there. Everyone brought their own chairs and the grandkids went to the pool. As we sat around Seymour, we started the barbecue and cooked hamburgers and hotdogs. We decided on a light meal tonight. It was nice sitting around visiting with each other.

"Well folks I guess this will be our last campfire on our vacation." Frank pondered. Frankie said, "We saw a lot of different landscape and James learned how to chase chicken. James, do you remember how much fun you had?" James replied as he laughed, "I guess none of us will forget. I felt sorry for that poor old farmer having a flat tire and the truck turning over and all the chickens escaping and going everywhere. I wonder how many he lost. I'm just glad it turned out ok, there were a lot of good people helping him."

It was fun to listen to all the stories; it's even more interesting to hear each of them tell their own side. I told them my favorite was going on Styles research ship. Daniel and Tina said at the same time, "I wish we could have gone with you guys. I had to agree, I wish all the kids could of went with us, maybe when they get older.

The three youngest one said they liked going into the cavern. They just wish they could have touched the stones. That reminded me about their rock collections. When I asked them about it, they jumped up and said, "We'll show you, and off they ran to get them. Maria and Twila looked at me and said, "You had to ask," as they got up to go after them. They had put the rocks up on a top shelve in the trailer. They needed to get them down before the girls started climbing up the cabinets to get them.

Dennis and James said, "It was great seeing our families and spending time with them. Dennis also said, "It was great showing you guys all the garter snakes." He had told us before about how they migrated, but we didn't know how many there were, it was pretty amazing. I had to agree with him. Seeing is believing!

The evening was wonderful; it was warm and no bugs out for a change. I guess the fire helped with that. The girls came back with their collection of rocks. They knew what types each of the stones were, and what you could use it for. I guess the books we got them about mineral and their healing powers came in handy. The grandkids had gone over to the picnic table and played board games. The adults were just sitting around talking about all the adventures. What a great family we have, I guess I was smiling, because Frank asked, "What are you smiling so big about? I told him, This! What wonderful kids and grandkids we have. I hate to see it end, but we'll have more adventures to come.

Day 27
Last Day on our trip!

It's hard to believe this is our last day on our vacation. But it will be nice to be home. We both are looking forward to staying in one place for more than a couple of days. Funny, we already have plans to take the boat out next weekend. We want to do some fishing and scuba diving. We do miss the ocean.

All the grandkids wanted to ride with us on the last leg of our journey. The plan was to look at the pictures and pick out the ones they liked and we are going to make a memory board for each of them. As we went through the piles of pictures, I was surprise to see how many piles we had. I guess if you have eight cameras going, it shouldn't be a surprise. I know I took my fair share of them. I think I was making up for the time on Rosland Island, where we didn't have a camera. I can only imagine how cool it would have been to have a camera on the island. Granted we couldn't show them to anyone, well the ones of the Merbeings anyway.

After about an hour we had all the piles in order. We had put them in order of where we stop, going from first to last. Of course, we haven't developed the pictures from today. We'll do that when we get back to Houston.

The grandkids and I talked about the trip, and a picture would bring up a memory of something that had happens there. It's always interesting listening to the kid's side of the trip. Frank would put his two cents in once and awhile.

After awhile we stopped for lunch, we were in no big hurry to get home. We arrived in Houston a little after five, tomorrow we need to clean the rigs up and return Seamore back to Linda.

We unloaded all the food and clothes; we figure the rest can wait until tomorrow. We still live in Franks' guest house; we are normally out on our boat. But when we're on land we stay here. Twila and Maria had gone straight to their houses. They had told us they will bring the walkie talkie by tomorrow.

Frankie and Wanda were unpacking their van; their boys were hard at work putting everything in its place. We squared Seamore away, Frank is going to wash it tomorrow and then fill the gas, water and propane tanks up too, before returning it to Linda and Jake. The floor didn't look that bad considering that we lived in it for a month.

We told the kids good night and went to the house. I took a long shower and crawled into bed. It was nice sleeping in our own bed again. While Frank is in the shower I wanted to close on the day. What a great adventure we had with our kids and grandkids. I hope it's something they will remember forever.

Well Frank's out of the shower, so I guess I'll close for tonight.

CHAPTER 24

July 15, 1969

We spent the morning cleaning the rest of Seymour up. It's a lot of work to wash a Class A rig. It was nice to have the grandkids helping us. It was great fun, of course, there was a few water fights and a couple of sponge fights. I may have been the instigator of one of the sponge fights.

After lunch we took Seamore back to Linda and Jake. They were surprised to see it so clean. They asked us how our trip was. Of course, we had to tell them all about it and what a wonderful time we had.

We got back to the house, around 4 o'clock. We went over to visit Frankie and his family; they were sitting out at the pool. We joined them for little while, and then we headed back home to our little cabin.

It was nice having time to ourselves. We laid around and did some reading and writing. Then we watched a couple of new TV shows that were out, Rockford and Emergency. We're looking forward to going out on our sailboat this weekend. The kids can't go, so we decided to just sail down to Corpus Christi by ourselves. We wanted to get some fishing and scuba diving in. The Bay is wonderful for that type of thing. It will be really nice to be out on the boat again, and enjoying the water. The weather is supposed to be really nice, warm and with a light breeze. We have already packed everything we will need to take back to the boat.

I decided to start putting the dates in my journals, because I am not writing in it as often as I used to. Day-to-day entries get kind of boring after a while. If you're not on an adventure, there isn't a lot to write about.

July 16, 1969

We had a great time on the boat this weekend. The weather was warm, with a light breeze. We caught dinner and did some scuba diving. We ran into some friends that we haven't seen in a while. They had wondered where we had been. George said, "We thought you may have gotten lost again!" Frank laughed and told him about our trip. George is an old friend of ours, from the military days; he pretty much lives on his boat, and is single. He is more of Frank's friend than mine; I think he is kind of weird!

The rest of the evening we went over to some other friend's boat and played some cards. We ended the night around 10. Frank was asleep before his head hit the pillow.

July 17, 1969

We got in late last night, so I slept in late, but I did sleep like a rock. Frank was already gone when I woke up. He didn't tell me where he was going. So I was surprise that he wasn't there when I went looking for him. I walked over to Frankie's house to see if he was over there and he wasn't. Frankie had a big grin on his face which always meant something was up. I tried to get it out of him, but he wasn't having anything to do with it. He just told me, "Dad will tell you when he gets back!" I went looking for Wanda; I figured I could get it out of her. But she wouldn't have anything to do with it either. When I looked at the boys, they took off running and plug their ears. As if they couldn't hear me.

Frankie told me, to be patient and I'll see soon enough what Dad was up to. So I went back to the house and waited for Frank to come home. I had no clue what he was up to.

When he opened the door to the house, two little dogs came running through the door. The first thing they did is jump on my lap and wiggled their little butts like they were my best friends. I couldn't believe it, that Frank went and got the dogs that we had looked at earlier this week.

They were both mutts one was black and white, and one was brown and white. The dog pound said they were a terrier mix, and there's a little bit of something else in them. They were both girls, they must've weighed about 12 pounds each. They are sisters; their names are Sheba and Susie. They are just so full of love, and they want to share it with us.

I looked at Frank and he said, "Well, you said you wanted a dog, now we each have one! Now all we need to do is get a RV, so we can travel around this country of ours!"

I turned to our new pets, Sheba and Susie, well what do you think? Do you think you will like traveling around in a RV. They started wagging their tails and jumping around. I looked at Frank and told him I guess that mean yes! Frank agreed, and replied, "Let's go tell the Frankie and family. I'm sure they will like this idea better than us going out on our boat trip. I had to laugh, as I told the dogs come on, let's go meet the family. They ran to the door and started barking. I guess we were not moving fast enough for them.

We didn't even get to Frankie's house before our grandsons were there picking up the dogs. I think they were waiting for us. They already knew about the dogs, their Grandpa had told them what he was up to. So it wasn't a surprise for them.

We told Frankie and Wanda about our plan to get a RV and start traveling around the country. The first thing Wanda said was, "Good, it is better than going on an ocean trip. Frank smiled and said, "I told you so! I just smiled and agreed.

Frankie wanted to know when we would be going shopping for the RV. He said, "When you do, let me know, I want to go! I spoke up and said how about tomorrow. We all agreed that would work. Frankie said, "I can't wait to see what my sisters say. You know they're going to want to go with you." Yea, but they can't maybe they can join us once and awhile.

We called the girls and told them of our plans, next thing we knew we were all having dinner talking about where we will be going next. Here we go again!

July 22, 1969

Well we did it! We purchased us a trailer, instead of a Class A. I learned more about RV's then I ever wanted to know. Frank had done the research as usual. We had brochures everywhere, on every type of rigs there was.

Our trailer is thirty feet long; it has two doors, one at each end. We even have a bedroom. It will sleep six, the colors inside are blue and green, with a leaf design. We wanted to get a trailer instead of a Class A (which is what Seamore was) because if we want to do something we will have the truck to drive. We already had the truck anyway.

We did discover that there are a lot of campgrounds by the docks. I guess we're not the only old people that like to travel on land and water. Of course, we had to buy all kinds of new things to go with it. After going on our thirty day trip with the kids, we had a really good idea about what we needed.

We purchased a United States map for the side of our trailer. Frank and I had a discussion about if we should fill in the ones we went thought with the kids. We finally agreed to fill them in, mostly because we had no plans of going that direction for a little while.

We invited the grandkids over for a camp out; we had parked the trailer by the house. But that didn't stop us; we had a great time with them. We talked about our trip and about going fishing in the morning. It's been a while since we have been out on the boat. Enola and Treva had gone to a Rock show with their parents. They had brought the stone they had gotten from the show. Enola showed us her bags she had gotten to hold her wonderful stone. We had purchased a telescope, so the kids was taking turns using it. Tina said she saw a UFO by the moon. Of course, all the kids had to see it. I never did! We finally send the grandkids to bed, they all slept in tents. Frank and I slept in our new trailer. We're getting way too old to be sleeping on the ground.

I guess we'll be going on a test run, later this month. We're going to stay in Texas for the first month. That way we can still use our sailboat too. Twila and Dennis said they would sail it to where we what it and then just take it home. The other kids said they would too, if we wanted them too.

It's going to be an interesting change for us. I think the hard part will be missing our kids and grandkids. But when they are out of school, they will join us. With both of us in our early 60's, we figure we have a good ten years to travel where ever we what to. We both what to do some rock hounding and work in fossil digging.

Well I guess it is time to close this journal, and start a new one for the next adventures we will have.